Also by Graham Masterton

A Terrible Beauty

Available from Pocket Books

Unspeakable

Graham Masterton

POCKEY STAR BOOKS
New York   London   Toronto   Sydney

An *Original* Publication of POCKET BOOKS

A Pocket Star Book published by
POCKET BOOKS, a division of Simon & Schuster, Inc.
1230 Avenue of the Americas, New York, NY 10020

ISBN: 0-7434-6294-7

First Pocket Books printing February 2005

10 9 8 7 6 5 4 3 2 1

POCKET STAR BOOKS and colophon are registered
trademarks of Simon & Schuster, Inc.

Cover design by John Vairo Jr.; cover photos
Richard H. Johnston/Getty Images; Jed Share Photonica

Manufactured in the United States of America

For information regarding special discounts for bulk purchases,
please contact Simon & Schuster Special Sales at
1-800-456-6798 or business@simonandschuster.com.

To my grandson Jake
and his grandmother Wiescka
with love

Poor Richard's

For her thirty-third birthday, Holly's boss, Doug, took her to Poor Richard's on Northeast Thirty-ninth and Broadway. Katie came along, too, of course, since she was not only Holly's case director but Doug's "significant other."

It was a Tuesday evening so the special was steak and snow crab, which was Holly's favorite, although Doug always swore by the tenderloin, medium rare, with a deep-fried onion blossom on the side.

The restaurant was crowded and noisy, so that they had to shout to make themselves heard. "Who's the Long Island Iced Tea?" yelled the server. Holly raised her hand and he passed it over. "Who's the Fuzzy Navel?"

Doug raised his beer glass and said, "Here's to Holly . . . the sweetest girl in the Portland child welfare service. May your days be blessed with sunshine and may your nights be filled with thrills."

"*Doug*—" Katie protested, but Holly shook her head and laughed.

"Don't worry. Just because I'm thirty-three and un-attached, that doesn't mean that I'm going to be living like a nun forever."

"I don't know why you broke it off with Eugene," said Katie. "I know he wasn't exactly Brad Pitt, but he wasn't Quasimodo, either."

"Yes . . . Eugene . . . ," said Doug. "I *liked* Eugene. It struck me that he was always so considerate."

Holly kept on smiling—that tight, determined smile she always put on when other people tried to order her life for her. "I wasn't looking for *considerate*," she said. "I was looking for *impetuous*. I was looking for *wild*. Besides, Eugene wore garters."

"*Garters?* Oh my God. You never told me that."

The server brought their starters: shrimp sauté for Holly, teriyaki chicken strips for Katie and Doug. "You want dip? Blue cheese? Lemon mayo? Tomato and honey?"

"He had a phobia about showing his legs because they weren't very hairy. He said they looked like a girl's."

"Hey, we can't all be gorillas."

Over in the dark, oak-paneled bar, more than fifty feet away, a bleached-blond woman in a shiny green cocktail dress was leaning toward a man with a short, iron-gray crewcut. "I have champagne in the icebox," she was saying. "Well, not real champagne but sparkling wine. We could kick off our shoes and drink sparkling wine and dance."

Her companion flapped his hand dismissively. "I don't want to kick off my shoes and drink sparkling wine and dance, okay? I'm fine here. I'm totally . . ."

He searched for a word, but all he could come up with was "fine."

The woman leaned even closer and started to play with the man's earlobe. "You don't know what you're missing. I could make all of your wildest dreams come true."

"I don't have any wildest dreams. I don't even have any tamest dreams."

The woman stroked his cheek. The man raised one finger and the bartender poured him another shot of Jack Daniel's.

"Do you know who you remind me of?" the woman purred.

"No, who do I remind you of?"

"Burt Lancaster, when he was younger."

"Burt Lancaster's dead."

"But you remind me of him. Like, *all man*, you know? Quiet, but all man."

The man tossed back the Jack Daniel's and raised his finger again.

A little farther along the bar, two men in crumpled business suits were talking and laughing. One of them was saying, "So this seventy-year-old guy is sitting in bed reading, okay? And his wife flings open the bathroom door and she's standing there bare-ass naked, okay, and she shouts out, 'Super pussy!' The old guy doesn't even look up. He just turns the page in his book and says, 'I'll take the soup, please.' "

Right in the far corner, sitting at a small table with a hammered-copper top, Holly could see two men drinking beers. One of them had his back to her, and because of the red-shaded table lamp, all she could see of his companion was the lower part of his face. He was talking quickly and quietly, and endlessly feeding himself with smoked and salted almonds.

"—depends when you want it done. I don't know. It's your decision. Whatever you decide, I'll work around it. But you have to make up your mind, you know? And once you've made up your mind, that's it, there's no going back. Because once I've told the guy, once I've told him, he's not going to be in contact anymore, he's going to vanish, *piff*, and I can't call him up at the last minute and say, 'Sorry, the client's changed his mind,' you get me?"

The woman in the shiny green dress was trying to stick her tongue in the man's ear and he kept flinching away from her.

"Listen, I washed my ears before I came out, okay?"

"Don't you like being licked? I could lick you in places you didn't even know you had."

"Give me a break, will you?"

"Why don't you take me home and let me find out where you like to be licked the most."

Doug was already looking flushed. He had peppery hair and a freckly complexion and it took only two glasses of Bridgeport ale for his neck to turn crimson. Katie was dark and pale, with iron-gray streaks in her shoulder-length hair, and whenever *she* drank she pushed her wire-rimmed glasses onto the end of her nose and became very, very meaningful.

"We were thinking, Holly, you know, that maybe you could use some more social interaction."

"You mean I need to get out more?"

"I mean try new people. Broaden your acquaintanceships."

"—so this Japanese tourist goes to the bank to change his yen into dollars, right?" said the joker at the bar. "And he says, 'What's going on, I got a hundred dollars yesterday, now you've only given me ninety-six. Why's that?' And the bank teller says, 'Fluctuations.' So the Japanese says, 'Yes, and fluck you Americans too.'"

"We're going out to Mirror Lake this weekend. We were wondering if you were interested in coming along. Doug hasn't been salmon fishing in months, and I just feel like getting out of the city."

"Just us three?"

"Well . . . I was thinking of asking Doug's friend Ned. You know, it's always better when it's a foursome."

"Have I met Ned?"

"I don't think so. No, you haven't. But you'll really like him."

"He's a really terrific guy," Doug put in. "Great sense of humor, you know. Great practical joker."

"You'd really like him. He used to play quarterback for Portland U. He's done pretty well for himself in the wood pulp business. And I can guarantee that he doesn't wear sock suspenders."

The man at the table in the corner said, "—you just let me know exactly where she's going to be, and when, and we'll take care of the rest. Don't go variegating your routine. Stay in town and have the cat sense not to do anything that's different from what you normally do. That's the mistake that so many clients make. They have a perfect story but for no reason they do something out of character, and that gets the cops asking themselves why did this guy do something out of character—cops being professionally nosey, which is what they're paid for."

He said something else, and by the way he curled his lip it looked like something of a threat, but Holly couldn't quite catch it.

"Oh, come on," said the woman in the shiny green dress. "We'll have a ball. I promise you won't regret it."

"All right. All *right*. You win. Shoes off, sparkling wine, licking, whatever you want. No dancing, though. Definitely no dancing."

"But I *like* to dance."

"Listen, I'll be lucky if I can stand up, forget about dancing."

"Then maybe we should leave it."

"What do you mean? I said yes, didn't I? You've been nagging me all evening and now you want to leave it?"

"I know, but you're drunk. Maybe we should leave it till you sober up."

The man turned and looked at her for the first time. "I don't think it would be a good idea to wait until I'm sober, because you don't turn me on when I'm sober."

Holly laughed. The woman heard her laugh and turned around, frowning, but Holly was obviously too far away to have overheard what she was saying, and she turned back to the man again, looking cross.

"Lipreading again?" said Doug, sucking teriyaki sauce from his fingers.

"Yes. I know I shouldn't."

"Look, how about Mirror Lake?" Katie persisted. "We can swim, we can take the boat out."

"And what else? Matchmaking 'round the old campfire?"

"Holly, it's just that I care about you. You're special."

Holly kept on smiling. "Let me think about it, okay? But just because I happen to be deaf, that doesn't mean that I need you to find lovers for me."

"Did I say anything about lovers? Doug, did I say anything about lovers?"

Holly glanced over to the table in the corner. The man finished his beer and wiped his mouth with a neatly folded paper napkin. "—there won't be a trace, I guarantee it. You won't even know she ever existed. How? You don't want to know how. In fact, the less you know, the better. But this guy's a pro. You won't be turning on the news to hear that somebody's found her detached head in a bus-station locker."

A Meeting with "Mickey Slim"

Mickey was waiting for her outside the restaurant, lounging back in his shiny black Oldsmobile Aurora, smoking a cigarette, which he tossed out onto the sidewalk as soon as he saw her.

She said good night to Doug and Katie. "That was great. I had such a good time."

Doug checked his watch. "You sure you don't want to come on to C.C. Slaughter's? Jesus, it's only a quarter after nine."

"I'd love to, but I'm really tired. Daisy has a math test tomorrow and I have to see the Joseph family at nine."

"Oh, the Josephs. . . . Okay, you'll need all of your strength for that."

She kissed them and gave them a wave as they walked away. Then she crossed the sidewalk to the Oldsmobile. Mickey leaned across the seat and un-latched the door for her.

"How's the sexiest public servant in the Pacific North-west?"

"A year older. It's my birthday today."

"Hey, why didn't you tell me? I would have bought you something. One of those magic Tillamook neck-laces you like so much."

"You police detective, me social worker. Let's keep it strictly professional."

"But I love you."

"No you don't. You only love you."

Mickey was skinny and rangy and almost always wore a black suit and a black shirt with a black necktie. He would have been the first to admit that he wasn't partic-ularly handsome. His cropped black hair was receding and he had a sharply pointed nose, but he had wounded gray eyes and a kind of etched, half-starved look that seemed to appeal to almost all of the women he met.

His real name was Mickey Kavanagh, but years ago one of his sergeants had christened him "Mickey Slim"—not just because he was so thin, but in honor of the 1950s down-and-outs' cocktail of choice, gin mixed with DDT, which had the effect of being an upper and a downer at the same time. Which pretty much summed up Mickey's personality to a T.

"Thanks for that text message," he told Holly, hold-ing up his cell phone. "Those guys you were lip-reading . . . are they still inside?"

"No, they left about ten minutes ago."

"Get a look at them?"

"Not very clearly. The one who was doing most of the talking was forty-five, maybe, broad shoulders, long gray hair tied back in a ponytail. Craggy kind of face, if you know what I mean. Acne scars. His accent wasn't local: The way he was biting the ends of his words, I'd say that he was almost certainly out of Chicago. He used the words *cat sense,* too, and you very rarely hear anybody outside of Chicago saying that."

"What about the other one?"

"I never saw him speak. He had his back to me most of the time but he looked as if he were older, more stooped, you know? He was wearing a green raincoat and he was carrying a yellow plastic shopping bag. I think he may have had a mustache."

"Want to tell me exactly what was said?"

"It was very oblique, most of it. But I'd definitely say that they were arranging to kill some woman. The guy with the ponytail said that he was going to get a real pro to do the job. He said, 'You won't even know she ever existed.' "

"Want to come back to headquarters and look at some pictures?"

"This is my birthday, Mickey, and Daisy's waiting up for me."

"I'll make it up to you, I promise. I'll take you out to McCormick and Schmick's tomorrow night and then we can go back to your place and make love until the steam comes out of our ears."

"Sorry, Mickey."

"All right, we can go back to *my* place and make love until the steam comes out of our ears. You'll just have to be careful not to kneel in the cat litter."

"I'll look at some pictures at home, okay? And if I see a face that rings a bell, I'll call you."

"Okay, okay. I know when I'm spurned."

The Three Concubines

They drove through the brightly lit center of Portland, along the tree-lined transit mall, where people were still strolling between the flower tubs, window-shopping. It had rained earlier, but now the evening was dry and warm, although the lights from the stores and the streetlights and the forty-story Interstate Bank Tower were still reflected in the sidewalks.

"Been busy?" Holly asked Mickey.

"Are you kidding me? Those missing women are driving me nuts."

"No leads?"

He shook his head. "We still don't know for sure if they're in any way connected. I know they were all successful professional women, all four of them, and they all disappeared without telling their husbands or their friends where they were going. But until at least one of them shows up . . ."

"Any theories?"

"Personally, I think they all decided that their family responsibilities were holding them back and that the simplest thing to do would be to walk out the door and never come back."

"You think they *all* did that, independently of each other? That doesn't seem very likely."

"Why not? One walks out, the others see it on the news and think, *What am I doing here with this Homer Simpson of a husband and these snotty ungrateful kids? I could do that.*"

Holly shook her head. "I'm not so sure. I know *men* walk out on their families sometimes."

"Why not women? Sarah Hargitay ran a very successful real estate business; Jennie McLellan had a thriving patisserie; Kay Padowska was a senior manager at First Portland Bank; and Helena Carlsson was a big noise in the Port Authority. All dominant, single-minded women."

"I'm a dominant, single-minded woman, but I wouldn't just walk out on my life."

"That's because you'd miss me too much."

"Are you kidding? I'd miss you like I miss hay fever when it starts to rain."

Ahead of them they caught sight of three burly women in red, blue, and yellow cheongsams, with high collars and slit skirts, tottering arm in arm along the mall together. Mickey put down his window and called, "Hey, girls!"

They came tripping over in their little silk Chinese slippers. Their faces were caked with thick layers of dead-white rice powder so that their five-o'clock shadows were covered, and their eyebrows were plucked into thin, startled arches.

"Lieutenant *Kavanagh!* What a wo-oh-onderful surprise!"

"Did you get that job at Embers Avenue?"

"Are you *kidding* me?" shrilled the girl in the blue cheongsam.

"They were so cruel to us, you don't have any idea," added the girl in the red cheongsam. "They were *beasts*."

"They said, 'Who are you supposed to be, *The Three Stooges Meet Fu Manchu?*'"

"Hey, you'll get over it," said Mickey. "You know you've got talent. When I saw you three singing 'Getting to Know You' that time . . . what can I say? Whoa, unforgettable."

"Who's the car candy?" asked the girl in the blue cheongsam, nodding toward Holly.

"Oh, I'm sorry. This is a good friend of mine, Holly Summers. She's a caseworker for the Portland Children's Welfare Department. One of the city's finest. Holly, this is Lotus Flower, August Moon, and Bruce."

"Good to meet you, honey," said Lotus Flower, reaching into the car and gripping Holly's hand. "You just watch this guy: He's got a reputation with us women."

They drove on. "Some characters, huh?" Mickey remarked. "Portland, City of Roses? More like the City of Fruits."

A Birthday Wish

Daisy was already in her pink Barbie pajamas when Holly turned the key in the door. She was sitting at the kitchen table with a mug of hot chocolate, watching television. Marcella, the nanny, was standing at the sink, washing dishes.

"Hi, Ms. Summers. You came back early."

"I guess I was a little tired, that's all."

"Hi, Mommy. Did you have a good time?"

Holly kissed Daisy on top of her head. Daisy was eight and a half, both pretty and gawky at the same time, all arms and legs, with long blond hair and a snubby little nose. She had her father's eyes: blue as bellflowers and with the same sparkle of suppressed mischief. For Holly's birthday, Daisy had made her a scrapbook crowded with pictures cut from magazines, recipes, poems, and Polaroid photographs that she had taken of places they had visited together, like the Japanese Garden and the Oregon Zoo and Multnomah Falls. It must have taken her hours and who could guess how many bottles of glue, and Holly had been so touched that her eyes had filled up with tears.

"You want a hot chocolate?" asked Marcella.

"No, thanks, Marcella. I think I could use a glass of wine. I have some work to do on the computer."

"Won't you be able to test me, then?" said Daisy brightly.

"I have some work to do on the computer *after* I've tested you."

"All right I go now?" said Marcella, hanging up her apron.

"Oh, sure. And here's your money for last week. Sorry it's late."

"You don't worry, Ms. Summers. I would look after Daisy free and for nothing, you know that."

Finding Marcella had been a godsend. She was forty-five, Italian, small and plump, with sweet, doll-like features and tiny hands and feet, like a Madonna figure from a church altar. Her three sons had all grown up and left Portland and her husband Luigi had been taken by lung cancer. ("He smoke like Mount Saint Helens.") Holly had met her when she moved into her third-story apartment on top of the Tor-refazione Restaurant in the Pearl District. Marcella had been working in the restaurant kitchen, and she had offered to keep an eye on Daisy while Holly struggled up and down the stairs with cardboard boxes and suitcases and clothes. After that she had agreed to look after Daisy every afternoon, after school. She called Daisy *mia bomboletta*, meaning "my little fritter."

Holly opened the fridge and took out a bottle of Duck Pond chardonnay. She poured herself a large glass and then sat at the kitchen table and kicked off her shoes.

"Did you have a cake?" asked Daisy.

"Uh-huh. I had bread-and-butter pudding with three candles in it."

"And did you make a wish?"

Holly took hold of Daisy's hand. "Sure I made a wish. But I can't tell you what it is or it won't come true."

Not only that, she didn't want to tell Daisy what her wish had been: that five-year-old Daniel Joseph wouldn't have to suffer anymore. Daisy knew all about Holly's work, but she wasn't yet old enough to understand the mundane horrors that parents are capable of inflicting on their own children. Yesterday afternoon at four forty-five Holly had been called to a house in Happy Valley where a mother had pressed her six-year-old daughter's hand onto a sizzling skillet and kept it there for over ten seconds. The reason? "She said wicked things. She said my brother kept touching her under her nightdress and she didn't like it. My brother would never do a thing like that." Her brother was twenty-nine, with two convictions for theft and aggravated assault.

Portland's Most Wanted

Like Holly, Daisy had always found math difficult, and it took over an hour for her to answer all the questions in her test paper. Holly felt sorry for her, because she could remember sitting alone at the back of the class when everybody else had finished their tests and gone out to play, tearfully trying to understand why 248 and 507 didn't add up to 779.

The trouble was, numbers didn't look like numbers. She thought that 2s looked like swans and 4s like sailboats and 8s like hourglasses, and how could you possibly add up swans and sailboats and hourglasses?

At last it was time for Daisy to go to bed. She had a small room directly opposite the converted bedroom that Holly used as her office. It had flowery pink-and-green wallpaper and flowery pink-and-green drapes and her pink-painted bed was covered with a patchwork quilt that Holly had bought at a secondhand store on Everett called Quilty Party. On top of Daisy's desk stood a jostling throng of Barbies: ballet Barbies, beach Barbies, walking-the-poodle Barbies, headless Barbies, one-armed Barbies, and Barbies dressed up in clothes that Daisy had cut out herself from cotton scraps (she wanted to be fashion designer when she grew up). All these Barbies were Holly's only material concession to Daisy having no father.

"I feel sick," said Daisy, as Holly tucked her in.

"I know. That's because you have a math test tomorrow."

"No, I feel really sick. Like I'm going to hurl all over my pillow. I mean, *bleagghh*, all my meatballs, all my spaghetti, all my Jell-O, everything."

"That's because you have a math test tomorrow."

"I might have meningitis."

Holly laid a hand on Daisy's forehead. "You do not have meningitis, I promise you."

"AIDS, then."

She went into her office and switched on her orange Mac. Compared to Daisy's clutter, this space was sparse and cool and painted in plain magnolia, with only three decorations on the walls: a glaring Tillamook mask made out of varnished wood; a color photograph of Daisy two days after she was born, with Holly's parents; and a black-and-white photograph of Holly sitting with her feet in the glassy water of Ira's Fountain, with David sitting a few feet away, his Dockers rolled up to the knee, staring in alarm in the opposite direction as if he had just caught sight of his future walking toward him.

In this photograph Holly looked painfully young and vulnerable, her blond hair cropped like the young Mia Farrow, her thin knees knocked together. These days she cut her hair in a more businesslike bob, but there was still something of the same breakable quality about her.

Next to her desk stood a stark black iron standard lamp and a fig tree in a black-varnished basket, and that was all. Yet, somehow the room gave her away, almost as explicitly as a signed confession. It was almost too sure of itself.

She logged on to the Portland Police Bureau's Most Wanted page. She tilted back in her captain's chair as she scrolled through the mug shots, sipping her wine. One dumb-looking meathead after another, dozens of them, and they all shared the same look of bewilderment, as if they couldn't quite believe that they were human beings like the rest of us.

John Shine, thirty-seven, wanted for kidnap and homicide. Ernest Valdez, twenty-three, wanted for kidnap and rape. Leon Broughton, twenty-six, wanted for robbery, arson, and assault with a deadly weapon. Emily Card Venue, thirty-three, wanted for triple infanticide.

Anybody who didn't know much about children's welfare would have found it hard to understand what had led these faces to be wanted for such serious crimes. But Holly had seen too many little girls with third-degree burns on their hands, like the little girl in Happy Valley yesterday afternoon, and too many baby boys with maroon bruises on their cheeks and reeking diapers, and she knew exactly why these people couldn't quite believe they were human beings and why they resented the rest of the world so deeply.

An instant message rose up on her screen.

"Good evening, Holly. Sorry to introduce myself this way. My name's Ned Fiedler. Doug tells me he mentioned me at your birthday dinner tonite. And, btw, happy birthday."

"Hello Ned," Holly typed back. "What can I do 4 U?"

"Maybe I'm being too pushy here Holly but I'd VERY much like it if you could join us at the lake this weekend."

"Don't think I can make it Ned. I have a whole lot of work 2 catch up on. Laundry too."

"Well, can I respectfully ask you to consider it? From what Katie says, I'd really enjoy your company."

"OK, I'll think about it."

"You can contact me at fiedlerpulp@aol.com anytime. I'm waiting for your call. With bated breath."

Holly smiled and shook her head in disbelief. Men had come onto her in bars and restaurants and even in the office, but nobody had approached her by Hotmail before. She found herself wondering what he looked like. Short and fat, probably, with a drape-over hairstyle, a shiny mohair suit, and a personalized license plate saying WOODGOD.

She went back to the mug shots. Roman Fischer, forty-two, wanted for armed robbery. Christopher Friekman, thirty-four, wanted for narcotics offenses and extortion. Billy Positano, nineteen, wanted for rape, assault with a deadly weapon, and grand theft auto.

Then she stopped and scrolled back up again. On the right-hand side of the screen—although he looked fifty pounds thinner and his head was shaved—was the man she had seen talking in Poor Richard's this evening, she was sure of it. Merlin Krauss, fifty-two, wanted for extortion and attempted homicide. The same acne-eroded cheeks, the same jawline, but more important the same mouth that she had been watching so intently, with a question-mark-shaped scar on the left side of the upper lip. Holly could tell that he had actually been saying something when this mug shot was taken, because his upper teeth were lightly balanced on his lower lip, his lower lip was slightly rolled over, and his cheeks were drawn in. It was the letter F, and Holly could imagine the rest of the word.

She dialed Mickey's number and sent him a text message.

"Believe suspect Merlin Krauss."

There was a long pause, but then Mickey texted back.

"100 pc?"

"110 pc."

"Yr an angel. Talk 2 U 2mro."

For a long time Holly sat finishing her wine and staring at Merlin Krauss. *I wonder what made you what you are, Merlin,* she thought. *I wonder what nightmares you were brought up with. Or are you just what you look like, evil and stupid?*

Daisy's Nightmare

In the middle of the night, her bedroom door was hurled wide open and Daisy leaped onto her bed, sweaty and tangled up and shaking. Oh God. Holly put her arm tightly around her and then she reached over for the bedside lamp.

"What's the matter, pumpkin? What's happened?"

Daisy lifted her head so that her mother could see what she was saying. Her face was pale and her hair was stuck to her forehead. "I had a horrible dream. I dreamed that I woke up and I couldn't hear anything."

"Well, shush, don't you worry, that's never going to happen to you."

"It was like all these people were screaming at me and I couldn't hear anything at all, and they were all angry with me because I couldn't hear. They had black eyes with just holes in them and they kept screaming and screaming."

Holly gave her a squeeze and then she folded back the white loose-weave bedspread and allowed Daisy to

crawl into bed next to her. "There . . . you can stay with
me for a while. How about a glass of water?"

Daisy shook her head. "I was so frightened. It was
horrible."

"I know. But it was only a nightmare, wasn't it? And
it isn't the end of the world, being deaf. Even if they in-
vented a way of helping me to hear again, I don't think
I'd want to try it."

Daisy fiddled with the ribbons on Holly's nightshirt,
tying them into an elaborate knot. "Tell me when you
got deaf."

"Oh, come on. You know how I got deaf."

"I know but I like it when you tell me."

"It's a quarter of three in the morning, sweetheart,
and you have your math test tomorrow."

"But it won't take very long."

"Daisy . . ."

"Please, Mommy. If I go back to bed now, all those
screaming people with no eyes will come back."

Holly sighed. "All right, then. One day when I came
home from school I felt hot and I had a headache."

"No, no. Tell me about the house and the singing
lesson and the chicken pie."

Oh, well, thought Holly, and started to repeat the
time-honored version, word for word. "When I was just
about your age I used to live with my daddy and
mommy and my brother Tyrone in a tall, thin house on
Nob Hill. The house was painted cinnamon red and we
had a canary in a cage on the back porch that used to
whistle all day. One morning in April I went to school
and we had a singing lesson. I used to love singing. We
sang 'Green Grow the Rushes-O.' When I came home

my mommy had made chicken pie and that was my favorite, but I felt all hot and I had a headache and I couldn't eat more than a mouthful. My mommy took me upstairs to bed and then I was sick.

"I was sick again and again and my headache got so bad that I was screaming. My mommy gave me some Anacin and put me to bed, and that was the last thing that I remembered. When I woke up I was lying in the hospital, and my daddy was sitting in an armchair watching me. I said, 'Daddy, where am I?' and he got up from his chair and sat down next to me and gave me a cuddle and he was crying. I'd never seen my daddy cry before.

"I kept on saying, 'Where am I? Where's Mommy?' but he didn't answer me. It was then that I saw that his lips were moving but no words were coming out. I couldn't hear him talking, and I couldn't hear anybody walking around, and I couldn't even hear the bedsheets rustling. I said, 'Daddy, I can't hear you,' and I couldn't even hear myself saying it.

"It was like my head had filled up with water."

"You were very sad, weren't you?" said Daisy, prompting her.

"Yes, I was very sad. My daddy and mommy took me to an ear specialist but the ear specialist said that I would be deaf for the rest of my life. No more 'Green Grow the Rushes-O.' No more dogs barking or bells ringing or canary whistling on the back porch. And the strange thing was, I didn't just feel as if I couldn't hear, I felt *invisible* too. When people found out that I was deaf, they stopped talking to me. They even stopped *looking* at me, as if I had vanished.

"But my mommy didn't allow me to feel sorry for myself. She came from a strong family of Oregon pioneers who always believed that you had to make the best of things, no matter *how* lousy your luck."

Daisy nodded and softly said it with her: "No matter *how* lousy your luck."

"She took me for a walk along the Wildwood Trail one morning, when the sun was shining through the trees. She brought a picnic, and there was cold chicken pie. She held it up and said 'Chick-en pie,' very slowly and carefully, and pointed to her lips. Then she held up a bottle of Coke and said 'Coke.' I guess I'd already started to lip-read by myself, because I was so desperate to know what people were saying, but it was only then that I realized I could *learn* to lip-read better and better.

"After that I spent hours watching people talking on television, and when I was out shopping with my mother I used to stare at people's lips until they thought I was cracked.

"But one Saturday morning my father came downstairs and I could see him saying 'Where's my slippers, Claudine?' and I said, 'Under the couch.' Well, that was the second time I saw my daddy cry. He just stood in the middle of the living room and he burst into tears."

One Hell of a Day

The next morning it was raining—heavy, cold curtains which trailed across Portland from the northwest. After she had driven Daisy and Daisy's friend Arlo to school, Holly crossed the Burnside Bridge to the Southeast District. Below her, the Willamette River had the dull gleam of polished lead, and the tourists who were lining the decks of the sternwheeler paddleboats were all kitted out in bright yellow slickers.

Holly's windshield wipers flapped wildly from side to side but visibility was down to twenty feet, and like everybody else she had to drive at a crawl. Scarlet brake lights flared through the rain.

The Joseph family lived on Nathan Street, a short tract of shabby single-story houses with peeling paint and balding front yards and porches crowded with broken chairs and discarded stoves and sodden rolls of old carpet. As Holly parked her five-year-old Tracker outside the Joseph house, a young woman in a soiled pink bathrobe came out onto the porch of the house next door, smoking.

"Hell of a day," she said as Holly hurried across the yard.

Holly pressed the doorbell. The screen door had been kicked in and the paintwork around the doorknob was surrounded by a pattern of black fingermarks.

"That guy needs locking up," the young woman remarked. She had a face the color of unbaked pastry and straggly blond hair and she looked as if she hadn't eaten in a week, or had the appetite to.

"Well," Holly replied, pressing the doorbell again, "we try to give him all the help we can."

"Help? He doesn't need help. He needs locking up. He's a crazy person."

There was still no answer from Mrs. Joseph, so Holly opened the broken screen door and knocked. "Mary? Mary? It's Holly Summers!"

The girl blew smoke out of her nostrils. "Probably dead, from the noise that I heard last night."

"What kind of noise?"

"You know, noise. Banging, crashing, like somebody was throwing the furniture around and breaking all the dishes. Then screaming."

Holly knocked at the door again. "Mary! Can you hear me? It's Holly Summers! Come on, Mary, open up!"

"Probably dead," the girl repeated.

Holly took out her cell phone and texted Doug at the office:

"No reply at Joseph home. Neighbor reports domestic incident last nite."

There was a moment's pause and then Doug texted back:

"Check house then call in."

Holly pulled up the hood of her raincoat and stepped down from the porch. The girl watched her incuriously as she walked around the side of the Joseph house. An old brown armchair stood under the parlor window. Holly climbed up on it, balanced on one of the arms, and tried to peer inside. The gutter just above her was broken and a cascade of cold water clattered onto her hood.

All she could see inside the parlor was a half-open door, a rumpled green rug, and a tipped-over lamp with a fringed shade. There were broken plates, too, and a coffeepot without a handle. No sign of Mrs. Joseph or Daniel.

She stepped down into the seat of the armchair and the springs collapsed, trapping her foot between the cushions and pulling her shoe off. The girl next door shook her head and smiled and blew out smoke. Holly extricated herself, tugged her shoe back on, and then made her way around the back of the house. There was just as much rubbish there as everywhere else: the rusty cab of an old International pickup, a homemade dog kennel, bottles and crates and kitchen chairs with no backs on them. Next door, a huge brindled mongrel suddenly came running across the yard, barking at her. It crashed against the wire-mesh fence, which stopped it, but it continued to bark at her and throw itself against the fence again and again as if it wouldn't stop until it had broken through and gone for her throat.

She stepped up onto the rear patio, negotiating her way around a grease-encrusted K-mart barbecue and two orange-striped sunbeds that were spotted black with mold. The sliding glass doors that led into the kitchen were freckled with raindrops. She wiped them away with her hand and peered into the gloom.

At first she couldn't see anything at all except for the stove with dirty pots on top of it, and the sink heaped with dishes. In the corner, next to the breakfast bench, lay a heap of coats and blankets.

Then she saw movement and realized that somebody was hiding underneath the coats and blankets. She rapped on the glass and shouted, "Mary! Mary, can you hear me? It's Holly Summers! Mary, if you can hear me, come and open the door!"

There was a long pause. She didn't knock again but waited, so that Mrs. Joseph could see her standing there and see that she had come alone. Whatever had happened there the night before, Mary Joseph was obviously too terrified to let anybody in.

The rain continued to trickle down the window. Holly turned around and could see that the dog was still barking. At least its mouth was opening and closing, but as far as she was concerned it was barking in absolute silence.

Eventually, very slowly, the coats and blankets were lifted and Mrs. Joseph came crawling out from under them. She was a small woman, not much more than five feet tall, with a slack stomach and swollen ankles. Her tufty black hair was decorated with colored beads. When she stood up, gripping the breakfast bar for support, Holly could see that her reddish-brown shift dress was ripped at the shoulder so that part of her grubby white brassiere was exposed. Normally it was obvious that she was of Native American extraction, but this morning it was almost impossible to tell if she was human at all, let alone what kind of human.

Her face was swollen to twice its size, a Mardi Gras face painted in purples and crimsons and maroons. Her nose had been broken and her lips were split and encrusted with blood. She shuffled toward the window in one slipper and stood on the other side of the rain-spotted glass, trying to focus on Holly with eyes that were totally bloodshot.

"Mary, you have to let me in. . . . You need help!"

Mrs. Joseph continued to stand and stare, occasionally lurching on one foot to balance herself, a parody of an Indian medicine dance.

"Please, Mary, you have to open the door! Where's Daniel? Is Daniel okay? Come on, Mary, you have to open the door!"

At that moment the girl in the pink bathrobe appeared around the back of the house, holding a newspaper over her head to protect herself from the rain. When she saw Mrs. Joseph she said, "Holy shit. Holy fucking shit. I told you that guy was a crazy person."

"Call 911," said Holly. "Tell them what's happened. Here—phone this number too. That's my boss, Doug Yeats."

"We don't have a phone. Well, we did, but Ricky lost his job and everything."

"Well, here, take mine. Please, do it now."

"Okay. Okay. Jesus, look at the state of her. I mean I don't even *like* the woman, but, shit . . ."

Mrs. Joseph slowly lifted her hands toward the catch on the sliding glass doors. Her fingers were just as swollen as her face, so that she looked as if she were wearing thick purple gloves. She managed to nudge the lever upward a little and push the door back by an eighth of an inch, but then her hands dropped down to her sides and she stood looking at Holly helplessly, unable to find the strength to do any more.

Holly picked up a rusted spatula from the barbecue and slid it into the crack beneath the catch. She tugged it up once, twice, and then the catch clicked upward and the door slid open. She stepped into the kitchen just in time to catch Mrs. Joseph as she fell sideways toward the floor.

Daniel and the Devil

She laid her down on the heap of blankets. "Mary, can you hear me? Where's Daniel? I need to know where Daniel is."

Mrs. Joseph pointed with her broken left hand toward the living room. "Beating, beating, wouldn't stop."

Holly folded one of the coats to make a pillow and then she covered Mrs. Joseph with a blanket. "Try to keep still. The paramedics are coming; they won't be long. Where is your husband now? Where is he? Is he still in the house?"

Mrs. Joseph clutched at Holly's sleeve and she pulled Holly closer. Her breath was sour with bile. "He said . . . he said that Daniel had a devil. He said that he had to beat him, to beat the devil out. He beat him and beat him, and when I tried to stop him he beat me too."

"Where is he now?"

"He left, I think. I didn't see." She started coughing and she couldn't stop.

"Okay, Mary. Keep as still as you can. The paramedics are coming and the police are coming and you're going to be fine. I'm just going to look for Daniel."

Holly left Mrs. Joseph in the kitchen and walked through to the living room. The house was cold and gloomy and her shoes crackled on broken glass and fragments of china. Mrs. Joseph must have been serving a meal when her husband attacked her, because there was a broken ovenproof dish outside the living room door and trampled lumps of brown stew all over the carpet.

She wasn't an educated woman, Mary Joseph. She could read and write no better than a seven-year-old and she found it difficult to feed her family and keep her house clean, especially since her husband drank most of his welfare check. But her son Daniel was a gentle and bright little boy, inquisitive and sensitive. Holly had always believed that she had a good chance of saving him from the curse that afflicted so many Native American families in Portland: the curse of hopelessness and all the evils that went with it.

And there he was, lying on his back in the living room, where the curtains had been half torn down, and the couch tipped over, and most of Mrs. Joseph's precious china ornaments smashed. His blue-striped T-shirt had been pulled up around his neck and his short khaki pants had been pulled below his knees. One of his sandals was missing and his short white socks were spattered with blood.

Holly cleared away the broken china so that she could kneel down beside him. His eyes were closed and he felt very cold. He could have been sleeping: a moon-faced five-year-old with a flat Nez Percé nose, a little overweight, and very sallow, as if he were hardly ever allowed to play outside. There were no bruises on his cheeks but his shiny black hair was clogged at the top with dried blood, like a crusty beanie.

His body was even worse. His stomach was a mass of purple swellings, and there were livid diagonal lines across his chest, his upper thighs, and his genitals, scores of them, as if he had been furiously beaten with a cane or whipped with an electrical cord. Holly pressed her finger to the soft inside of his wrist, trying to feel for a pulse, but she couldn't. She laid one hand on his chest, wondering if she ought to start CPR, but she felt the crunching of broken ribs and was scared that she might do even more damage if she tried.

She bent over him as close as she could. She couldn't hear if he was breathing but might be able to sense his breath against her cheek.

"Please don't be dead," she whispered. "Daniel, can you hear me? Please don't be dead."

It was then that she felt a hand on her shoulder. It was a nudge at first, but then a shake, and another shake, even rougher. She turned around and looked up and there was Elliot Joseph, wearing jeans and a studded denim jacket, a black bandanna tied around his fraying gray hair, his eyes glistening with rage and drink.

"What the fuck are you doing here, you deaf bitch?"

Rule 33 (a)

Rule 33 (a) of the Portland Children's Welfare Department manual on dealing with belligerent parents. Stand up, making no sudden moves. Look the belligerent parent directly in the eye but not in a confrontational manner. Keep your hands by your sides. Speak soothingly and repetitively and try to appeal to the belligerent parent's sense of responsibility and self-esteem. For instance, do not say "What kind of a parent do you think you are?" Rather say, "I know you're a very good parent and I'm sure that you want the best for your child."

"Mr. Joseph, you're a very good parent," said Holly.

Elliot Joseph stared at her, blinking in amazement. "I'm a what? I'm a fucking *what?* I'm a fucking *outstanding* parent. You tell me—you *tell* me—what father would do for his boy what I did?"

"I'm not sure, Mr. Joseph."

"Oh, no? I'll tell you what any other father would have done. He would have let the devil go on growing inside of him, until it took over his *body* and his *soul* and eaten him alive! Any other father would have let him go on having nightmares for the rest of his— Jesus! Do you know what *nightmares* he was having?"

He staggered, almost losing his balance, and suddenly focused his eyes on Daniel as if he didn't know who the boy was.

"That's—*that's* Daniel! Jesus, that's my boy. What have you done to him? What the fuck have you done to him?"

"He's had an accident, Mr. Joseph. I've called the paramedics and they're on their way to help him."

"An *accident?*" Elliot Joseph pushed aside one of the armchairs and dropped onto his knees on the floor. Holly could smell the whiskey on him, and it made her eyes water. He lifted Daniel's torso and shook him. "Daniel! *Daniel!* Listen to me, boy, this is your dad! Daniel, you listen up, now!"

"Mr. Joseph, he's very badly hurt. I know that you don't want to make his injuries any worse."

But Elliot Joseph shook Daniel even harder. "Daniel, goddamnit! What's the matter with you? Are you trying to make me look like some kind of asshole?"

"He's hurt, Mr. Joseph. He has broken bones."

"Hurt? *He's* not hurt! Now, that devil, oh, yes! That devil got hurt okay! I beat the devil out of him! I beat it out! I saw it with my own eyes! It was black! It was like a black shadow! I saw it! I beat it out of him! I saved him! Daniel! Daniel, if you don't fucking open your eyes and look at me I'm going to beat the living shit out of you, boy, the same way I beat the living shit out of your devil! Open your fucking eyes!"

"He can't hear you, Mr. Joseph. Please leave him alone."

Elliot Joseph abruptly let Daniel drop back onto the floor. He gripped the edge of the armchair, missed it, gripped it again, and clambered onto his feet.

"He can't hear me? He can't *hear* me? Is that what you've fucking done to him? You've infected him! You've made him deaf, just like you, you bitch!"

He took one unsteady step closer, and then another. This was one time when Holly really wished she could hear, because she wanted to hear sirens. Elliot Joseph wasn't tall but he had a huge bony head, with angular cheekbones and widely spaced eyes and a flat wide-spread nose. His upper body was massive, like a buffalo's, even though his legs were so short. Mickey Slim had once described him as a "walking definition of threatening behavior."

"If anything happens to my boy . . . I'm warning you. I'll tear your fucking head off, you bitch, and I'll piss down your neck."

"Mr. Joseph, something has already happened to him. Something very serious. I can't even tell if he's still alive."

Elliot Joseph licked his lips. His eyes were wandering, as if he were trying to remember something important. Then he swayed forward even closer and whispered, "Do you know who I am?"

There was a clocksprung quality in the way he said it that made Holly feel seriously unnerved. She had come across it so many times before: the quiet, illogical, unanswerable questions, followed by a gradual escalation into total rage. It was the way that violent men justified what they wanted to do. *I'm trying to be reasonable here, you bitch, I'm trying to be calm, and all you can do is thwart me and provoke me. What else can I do but hit you?*

Even more softly now. "I said, do . . . you . . . know . . . who . . . the . . . fuck . . . I . . . am?"

Holly nodded but didn't reply. Whatever she said, it was going to be wrong.

"I am Hin-mah-too-yah-lat-kekt. That's my real name. That's my tribal name. Do you know what that means, Hin-mah-too-yah-lat-kekt?"

Holly shook her head.

"You should. It's one of the greatest fucking names in Nimipu history. It means Thunder Rolling Down From The Mountains, that's what it means. And I was given that name. I was *given* that name because I am a direct descendant of Chief Joseph, of the Wallowas, who was the greatest fucking—"

He stopped and frowned at her. "You don't give a shit about any of this, do you? You don't give a rat's ass."

"I'm worried about Daniel, Mr. Joseph, as I'm sure you are."

"You come here trying to break up my family . . . you come here bad-mouthing me. You come here making my boy deaf. You deaf bitch."

"Mr. Joseph, just take it easy. The paramedics won't be long now."

"You deaf bitch, look what you did to my boy! Look what you did to my house! That's all you ever wanted— wasn't it?—to break up my family and break up my house. Wasn't it? *Wasn't it?*"

Without any warning, he swung his arm and slapped her across the side of the head. Holly saw scarlet and her head sang, and she stumbled back against one of the upturned armchairs. Elliot Joseph came for her again, seizing the lapels of her raincoat and wrenching her from side to side.

"You deaf bitch! You deaf bitch! If you've killed my boy—"

He hurled her backward. She fell against the half-collapsed curtain pole and hit her hip against the windowsill. Elliot Joseph pitched the armchair out of the way and came for her, and she could tell from the way that his mouth was stretched open that he was screaming a high-pitched scream like a woman, as if he wanted to scream for her.

He tried to pull her up to her feet, but she deliberately allowed her knees to buckle, and he was so drunk that he toppled over her into the window bay. He managed to clamber up again and strike her on top of the head with his fist, but then he abruptly spun around and jumped away from her with all the agility of a cat.

He hadn't jumped, of course. He was far too drunk to jump. He had been bodily heaved away by Mickey Slim and another officer in uniform. Two more officers were already coming in through the door, followed by three paramedics.

Holly climbed to her feet. She was trembling and gulping for air. "Please—the boy. His name's Daniel. I don't even know if he's still breathing. His mother's in the kitchen . . . Mary. She's in a real bad way, too."

"Hey, hey, steady," said Mickey, putting his arm around her. His black raincoat was glittering with rain.

"All his bones are broken," said Holly. "Oh God. He's such a sweet little boy. He never did anything to anybody."

"I told you!" raged Elliot Joseph. *"I explained it to you! He had that devil in him! He had that devil in him and I had to beat it out of him!"*

"Will you kindly shut the fuck up?" snapped Mickey. Then he looked down at Daniel and asked the paramedic, "How is he? Is he still alive?"

"Hanging on by his fingernails. God knows how."

"Please," said Holly. "He's been through so much."

"We're doing what we can, ma'am. What's his pulse rate?"

"I saved him from the devil and you made him deaf, you deaf bitch!"

Mickey shot Elliot a quick look. Two of the officers had him in the doorway, holding his arms, while a third was handcuffing him. "Did he hurt you?" Mickey asked Holly intently.

"Just a—slap on the face. A knock on the head. Nothing serious." But the vision in her left eye was blurred and she was trembling like a startled pony.

"Okay," said Mickey, taking hold of her hand and giving it a squeeze. "I won't be a moment."

"It's all right. I'm not going anywhere until I know that Daniel's okay."

Mickey went across to Elliot Joseph. He kept his back turned to her, so Holly couldn't see what he was saying, but he nodded his head from time to time as if he were talking to Elliot Joseph quite calmly. Only the complicated jumble of anxiety on Elliot Joseph's face gave Holly any idea that Mickey might be threatening him.

Elliot suddenly threw himself wildly from side to side. "You can't touch me! You can't touch me and you fucking know it! You touch me—you lay one single finger on me, go on!"

Nod, nod, nod, from Mickey.

"I got rights. I got fucking human rights and tribal rights and you touch me, you just fucking touch me once, and you're finished. You and that deaf bitch who made my boy deaf. I'll get the both of you, I swear it."

Nod?

"You're out of your mind. That's my boy over there, and if I beat that devil out of him, you ought to be giving me a fucking *award*."

Nod, nod, nod?

"Well, she's my wife and she tried to stop me beating him and that was not in the boy's best interest, was it? If your boy had that devil in him, what would *you* do? Nothing, I'll bet, you faggot."

Nod.

"She had it coming. She dropped the fucking supper and she had it coming. A woman drops your fucking supper, what are you supposed to do? Say, like, 'Thank you very much, no problem, I'll just eat it off the rug'?"

Mickey turned to one of the officers. The officer's face was round and bland like a self-confident cheese, no eyebrows and tiny, colorless eyes. He unholstered his baton and handed it over. Mickey smacked the baton in the palm of his hand, *smack, smack, smack,* although Holly couldn't hear it.

"So what are you going to do?" Elliot Joseph demanded, defiantly lifting his chin. "Hit me? You better just try, you faggot. I got human rights and I got Wallowa rights."

Mickey gave no perceptible nod this time, but he must have said something because the cheese-faced officer suddenly reached up and seized Elliot Joseph's bandanna, wrenching his head back. Then he clamped his other hand around Elliot Joseph's throat.

"Wob you doib, mab, I carn breeb!"

Mickey took a step to the right. Elliot Joseph tried to purse his lips but he was gasping for breath and so he couldn't. Mickey tilted the baton way back over his shoulder, paused, and then cracked him straight in the mouth. Blood flew up against the door, and the cheese-faced officer flinched as his cheek was sprayed with scarlet squiggles.

One of the paramedics looked up from the floor. She glanced toward the doorway but didn't make any comment about what she saw there. "The kid's stable," she told Holly. "We should be able to move him now. Do you want to come along?"

Hard Words at the Doernbecher

It was well past five o'clock before Dr. Sokol came along the corridor to tell Holly that Daniel was going to survive.

She had been sitting for three and a half hours in the visitors' lounge at the Doernbecher Children's Hospital. She had started to type out her reports on her laptop, but her head was throbbing and she couldn't focus without squinting, so she closed it up. She knew that she should have gone home, but she couldn't—not if Daniel was going to die—and so she stood by the window while the rain gradually trickled down in front of her face, and lightning flickered in the distance.

Every time the lounge door swung open she looked up with a nervous jump. She knew that it couldn't be Elliot Joseph, but she couldn't stop herself. She had been jostled and punched plenty of times before, but Elliot had done more serious damage than a few bruises. He had made her question her competence. If she weren't deaf,

maybe she would have heard him muttering threats behind her back. Maybe she would have picked up some
subtle intonation in Mary's voice, some plea for help that
she simply hadn't been able to detect by lipreading.

The lounge door opened and Dr. Sokol appeared. He
wasn't much older than Holly and had a blue-shaven
head and rimless glasses. He was still wearing his green
theater robes and he looked exhausted.

"Well, it was touch and go a couple of times, but the
kid's going to live."

"How bad is it?"

Dr. Sokol wiped his neck with a towel. "About as bad
as you can get. Let me tell you, I've had to deal with
kids who were hit by semis, and even *they* weren't as
badly traumatized as Daniel. He has a skull fracture, a
broken collarbone, seven broken ribs, a broken pelvis,
a fractured ankle, a ruptured spleen, and a damaged
liver. That's not including all of his lacerations and con-
tusions."

"You say he's going to live. . . ."

"It's too early to say if he's going to make a compre-
hensive recovery. We had to relieve some pressure on
the brain tissues as soon as they brought him in, and in
the long term I'm worried about his mobility. His father must have used him as a trampoline."

"Jesus," said Holly.

Dr. Sokol lifted his finger and thumb, pinched only a
half-inch apart. "He was *this* close to the cemetery, believe me."

Holly didn't know what to say. Dr. Sokol sat down,
breathing with the deep steadiness of a man who was
doing his best to keep his self-control. Then he said, "I

thought Children's Welfare were supposed to keep an eye on situations like this . . . make sure that things like this didn't happen."

Holly sat next to him. "We try to do our best, Doctor. But we have very limited resources and very restricted rights. The law is overwhelmingly in favor of children being taken care of by their natural parents, and it isn't at all easy to define where careless parenting ends and calculated cruelty begins."

"Careless parenting? Elliot Joseph has a long-term history of alcoholic psychosis. He seriously believed the kid was possessed by a devil. Judging by Daniel's general condition, he must have been whipped and beaten several times before, over several months at least. What clearer definition of constructive cruelty do you need than that?"

"He was beaten before?"

"Pretty consistently, I'd say."

"I never saw any bruises . . . and his mother never said anything."

"I thought you people were trained to see the signs."

"I never saw any bruises, ever! My God! Don't you think I would have done something about it if I had?"

Dr. Sokol looked at her for a long time. He didn't say anything, but she could guess what he was thinking. She could also tell that she had shouted too loudly. When she shouted too loudly, her voice became even more distorted than usual. Her speech therapist had told her, and so had Daisy: "When you're upset, Mommy, you sound like you're drowning."

Mount Hood

The rain trailed away to the east, and the city sparkled in milky sunshine.

Holly stood by the window in the waiting room, watching Mount Hood reappear from the clouds.

Mount Hood was fifty-six miles away to the southeast, the tallest peak in Oregon, at 11,235 feet. Sometimes it looked to Holly like a mountain from a Japanese painting, snow-covered and spiritual, a place where the gods assembled. At other times it appeared more sinister, like a pyramid-shaped spaceship from *Stargate*.

But she felt its presence every day; she felt its overwhelming gravity; and sometimes, when she and Daisy were out cycling through Forest Park, she would stop, and shade her eyes, and stare at it, as if it were somehow the answer to what had happened to her, and where her destiny lay.

She would look at Daisy afterward and feel that extraordinary sensation of being a mother, of having created a daughter to go out into the world and do things that she would never do. Most of all—most precious of all—was that Daisy could *hear*, and when she saw Daisy clapping or dancing or listening to music, Holly was almost compensated for the total silence which always surrounded her.

Every day, winter and summer. Silence.

George Greyeyes Drinks Cappuccino

She was packing away her laptop and her report papers when George Greyeyes appeared in the waiting-room doorway.

"Holly? Hey, I've just been over at the Vets' Hospital: Doug told me I'd find you here." He came up to her and gave her a hug. He was six feet four inches tall and always made her wish she were wearing six-inch heels.

"I was just leaving, as a matter of fact."

"Are you *okay?* Doug told me that Elliot Joseph attacked you."

"A couple of bruises, that's all." She tried to smile but she was a little too close to crying, and all she could manage was a grimace.

"The nurse . . . told me about Daniel," said George. He always spoke very slowly, so she found it easy to read his lips. "I suppose we can thank our lucky stars that bastard didn't quite manage to kill him."

"Not much to be thankful for, is it?"

George checked his weighty stainless-steel watch. "Listen, how about you give me a ride back downtown and I buy you a coffee? I think we need to talk about this."

They left the Doernbecher Children's Hospital and Holly drove them into the city center. More rain was drifting in, and it speckled the windshield. George Greyeyes touched her arm to attract her attention. "Knowing you, I expect you think . . . this is entirely your fault."

She glanced at him. "Who else can I blame? I've had my suspicions for over six months that Elliot Joseph was beating up on Daniel's mother."

"Did you ever ask her direct?"

"Oh, for sure. She denied it—she *always* denied it. But whenever I made a visit, there was always an *atmosphere,* you know, especially when Elliot was prowling around. That thing with women when they fiddle with their jewelry and they won't look you in the eye and they keep repeating over and over that everything's just fine. My God, I've been doing this long enough. I should have trusted my intuition."

The rain suddenly started to grow heavier, and people on the sidewalks scurried for cover. They stopped at a red traffic signal and George touched her arm again. "There's nothing like hindsight, Holly, especially in the child welfare business."

"But it honestly never occurred to me that he was hurting Daniel too. Daniel always seemed so . . . well, he wasn't particularly *happy*—that was obvious—but he wasn't distressed."

"Detached, more like. Children have this way of accepting things, even abuse. After all, they don't have much of a choice, do they?"

"I never saw any marks on him. Never."

"Well, Elliot must have been clever at hiding it, like most abusers are. Punch them in the stomach, twist their ears, whip them on the buttocks with a wire coat hanger."

"But I didn't think the situation through, did I? I didn't ask myself *why* Elliot might have been hitting Mary. It didn't occur to me that she was trying to keep him away from Daniel."

"No reason why you should," said George. "If anybody's to blame, it's me."

"What do you mean?"

"Well, I knew that Elliot was hearing voices and experiencing psychotic episodes about demonic possession. I've come across it quite a few times before in Native American alcoholics. They get their tribal mythology all mixed up with their *delirium tremens.*"

George Greyeyes was forty-one years old, with high cheekbones and the classic Roman nose of the Nimipu, which was what the Nez Percé Indians called themselves. His shiny black hair was brushed straight back to his collar, and he always wore three-piece suits and two-tone shirts and black shoes as shiny as his hair. Instead of a necktie, however, he wore a silver necklace with a turquoise thunderbird on it.

He was a senior case worker for NICW, the National Indian Child Welfare Association, which was based in Portland—the only association in the country that dealt specifically with abused Indian children. He and Holly had known each other for more than eleven years. In fact, it was George Greyeyes who had persuaded her that she ought to look for a job in child welfare, and over the years they had worked together on dozens of cases, particularly Native American children with one or both parents in prison.

Holly and George had developed an unusual rapport, a calm and natural closeness in which conversation was rarely necessary. This was partly because of the mundane brutalities they encountered, day after day: daughters raped by their fathers, babies burned by their mothers' cigarettes, two-year-old toddlers starved and locked in cupboards for weeks on end. Most of the time, words weren't enough.

Holly parked opposite Peet's Coffee & Tea on Southwest Broadway. She and George dodged across the street under her red-and-white golf umbrella. Inside the coffeehouse it was warm and busy and smelled of freshly grinding arabica. Holly saw several people she knew from the Justice Center and gave them a wave. Then she and George took a table in the corner by the window. Holly ordered a skinny almond-flavored latte and George ordered a cappuccino with extra sprinkles. On the windowsill beside them stood a vase of yellow roses.

Holly pushed her hand into her hair. "God . . . this is the first time in thirteen months I could really use a cigarette."

"This wasn't all your fault, Holly, take it from me."

"No . . . Michael Sokol was right: I should have read the signs. I always suspected that Elliot might be violent. But, for crying out loud, I have *dozens* of cases where husbands are violent—even in the most respectable families—yet, they never touch their kids. A mother finally told me last Friday that her husband had been punishing her for years—like, ritual punishments for little things that she'd forgotten to do: put a fresh roll of toilet paper in the bathroom, maybe, or press the shirt that he wanted to wear. Two or three times a week he locked her in the bedroom, stripped her naked, and beat her with a cane while she had to beg his forgiveness for being such a bad wife. . . . And that was in Northwest, in the smartest six-bedroom house you've ever seen, with two Mercedes in the garage, and they had twin seven-year-old girls that the husband *doted* on."

George had hands as big as tractor seats, and he made a mess of tearing open a packet of brown sugar. "Sometimes you can't read the signs because you don't know what the signs mean. That's why I'm telling you that *I'm* to blame too. I went to interview the Joseph family only seven weeks ago, and I could see then that Elliot was severely delusional, and getting worse."

"I saw your report. That's another reason why I feel so guilty."

"Uh-huh. Don't be. You couldn't see what he was delusional *about*. Like I say, many Native American alcoholics have nightmares based on ancient Indian beliefs. Your *white* alcoholic, okay, he hears voices and he sees bugs climbing up the walls—frightening enough, I'll grant you. But your Native American alcoholic sees really *primal* terrors: monsters and devils that are deeply ingrained in his tribal psyche. I had one guy who insisted he was being followed by the Eye Killers, who can stop your heart just by staring at you; and another guy who was thought that Bear Maiden was hiding under his bed. Bear Maiden is supposed to be covered all over in black hair, and she can break your neck with one bite.

"It seems more than likely to me that Elliot Joseph believed Daniel was possessed by a Native American devil. I don't know which one."

Holly said, "He kept saying it was black, like a shadow."

"Could have been Raven. Raven is usually a bird, but he can take on any shape he feels like. Traditionally he's very cunning and dangerous, a scavenger. But whatever devil it was, it obviously scared Elliot so much that he felt he had no other choice except to exorcize it. That was a danger I should have anticipated and warned you about."

He took his spoon and scooped the froth off the top of his cappuccino. "I just want to say this, Holly: You and I, we were partly responsible for what happened here, I'll admit it, but it was a very unusual incident, very difficult to predict, and we went through all the correct procedural steps. I don't think that we should fall over ourselves to accept *all* the blame."

"It's just that I could have saved him," said Holly. "You should have seen him, George. He was all *broken.*" She was so upset that she couldn't say any more.

George reached across the table. On his right hand he wore a heavy silver ring with a profile of Chief Looking Glass embossed on it. "You're shaking."

"I'm a little cold, that's all."

"Holly . . . you don't have to be brave *all* the time. It's not an official job requirement."

"It's just that . . . Elliot Joseph . . . I don't know. I feel like he's tainted me."

George nodded as if he understood exactly what she meant. "The Nimipu have a saying, Holly: We all live in one another's shadow." He paused, and then he said, "Come on, you look beat. Finish your coffee and go on home. I can take the bus."

"Mickey Slim" Brings Lilies

At eleven A.M. the next morning, Holly was just about to go into a meeting with Doug and all the other department heads when Mickey appeared out of the elevators at the far end of the corridor carrying a huge bunch of white lilies wrapped in cellophane. He waved the lilies from side to side as if he were flagging down a train, and he shouted out something, but he was too far away for Holly to see what it was.

Katie said, "My *God*. He must have stolen those from the cemetery."

Mickey came jogging up to them, out of breath. "Hi! Holly! *Fwoff!* I just came by to see how you were! And to bring you these!"

"Those are for *me?*"

"Because of what happened yesterday. You know . . . you getting attacked like that."

"Oh."

Mickey raised his hand and gently touched her forehead, close to her hairline. "That's a heck of a bruise you've got there. Did you put an ice pack on it?"

"Frozen peas."

"Well, here," he said, and handed her the lilies.

"I'll catch up with you in a minute," she told Katie. Katie winked at her and went into the meeting.

"You, ah, how do you feel?" asked Mickey.

"Bruised. Battered. What do you think?"

"I heard that Daniel Joseph made it through surgery."

"Yes, he did."

"So he's going to be okay?"

"Probably not. There's only a twenty-five-percent chance that he's not going to suffer from some kind of physical impairment. Probably mental too. Cerebral edema."

"That Elliot Joseph. What a piece of shit. Excuse my language."

"Yes, well, I have to get into my meeting. Thank you for the flowers."

Mickey narrowed his eyes. "Do I sense some lack of warmth here?"

"Lack of warmth? I wouldn't call it that."

"No? What would you call it?"

Holly gave a defensive shrug. "I think I'm just surprised, that's all. Taken aback."

"Oh, yeah?" said Mickey, with an exaggerated expression of bafflement. "Taken aback by what exactly?"

"What you did to Elliot Joseph, what else?"

"I'm sorry, I'm not following you."

"You knocked his teeth out, Mickey. I couldn't believe it. You deliberately knocked his teeth out."

Mickey laughed in disbelief. "Holly, the man is an irredeemable psychopath."

"That didn't give *you* the right to act like an irredeemable psychopath too."

"He *hit* you, for Christ's sake. If we hadn't got there when we did, he probably would have killed you. I lost my temper, that's all."

"It didn't look to me like you were losing your temper. You looked completely calm."

"I'm always calm when I lose my temper. Chilled—that's me. The only time I get excited is when the Beavers are two games down."

"You still didn't have to knock his teeth out."

"Holly, there's one thing you have to understand. That piece of shit hit you, he hurt you, and as far as I'm concerned, if anybody hurts you—*anybody*—they're going to get hurt back. In spades."

Holly didn't really know what to say. All through her life she had always taken care of herself, and to have somebody else looking out for her was a strange experience. She didn't know whether she felt flattered or uneasy. Did Mickey feel protective toward her because he found her attractive, or because her deafness made her so vulnerable? Or an odd combination of both?

"Listen," he said, "if I upset you, I'm real sorry. The last thing in the whole world I wanted to do was upset you."

"No," she said, "I'm not upset. Not really. Not now. I can't say that I approve of what you did, but—well, I guess it was understandable."

"You're sure?"

"I'm sure. I could have ended up like Daniel, couldn't I?"

Mickey pressed his fingertips against his forehead, as if he were having difficulty thinking of the right words. "I don't usually . . . well, I don't want you to think that knocking people's teeth out is something that I'm in the habit of. But, you know, like W. C. Fields said, it's a hard world out there. It's amazing that any of us get out of it alive."

He looked up to judge her reaction. She said nothing, because she didn't really know what to say.

"By the way," he added, "Elliot Joseph comes up in court tomorrow. The DA is opposing bail, on the grounds that he's a continuing threat to his wife and son—and to child welfare staff too."

"Good," said Holly. "We'll be making a preliminary application to have Daniel taken into care."

Katie appeared in the doorway. "Holly, can you come in now, please? Doug's reading the minutes."

Holly turned to Mickey and said, "I really have to go. Thanks for the lilies."

"That's okay. You should have seen what they were charging for them, per bloom. Good thing I'm a cop and they give me a hundred-percent discount."

Holly laughed. She had been telling him the truth when she said that she liked him, but whenever he came close to her, she always felt as if she ought to be cautious, although she didn't exactly know why. She had met him nearly two years ago at the Children's Welfare Department barbecue, when she was holding a hot dog in each hand, one for her and one for Daisy, and she had liked the look of him even then. But she often felt that his eyes never quite agreed with what he was saying. She sometimes thought that there was a hidden "Mickey Slim," a very *watchful* "Mickey Slim," who very rarely showed himself.

"I'll talk to you later," she told him.

"You're really okay, though? I mean, Elliot Joseph hit you pretty hard, didn't he?"

"I'm okay."

"Okay, then. I'll see you later. Okay?"

The Ghost Boy

She was packing up her briefcase to leave when Katie came into her office. Katie was wearing a nubbly hand-knitted sweater in broccoli green and French mustard, and Holly knew that she was going to ask her something awkward because her head was tilted back and her glasses pushed right to the end of her nose. "Holly, I don't know if you're up to doing this. I mean, do tell me if you're not."

"Depends what it is. I'm in no condition to have a fistfight with anybody just at the moment."

Katie flapped a telephone message at her. "It's nothing much, just a backup call. A woman on Southeast Boise called the police just after ten o'clock this morning. She said she could hear a child screaming in the first-floor apartment right below her. The police attended and talked to Mrs. Hannah Beale. Mrs. Beale has an eleven-year-old son called Casper who is suffering from non-Hodgkin's lymphoma. According to Mrs. Beale, Casper doesn't want to undergo any more chemotherapy, and he was kicking up a fuss about it."

Holly checked her watch. Damn. She had promised Daisy that she would try to get home early.

"What would you like me to do?"

"I'd like you to check up on this situation, that's all."

"You mean today? Now?"

"It shouldn't take you more than twenty minutes. I wouldn't have bothered, normally, but one of the police officers reported that Mrs. Beale appeared to be very stressed-out."

"Okay . . . ," agreed Holly, reluctantly. She took the phone message and noted the address. Southeast Boise was over the river, on the opposite side of the city. She hoped that the afternoon traffic wouldn't be too clogged up.

She buttoned up her coat. On the windowsill beside her, in a tall sunlit vase, stood the lilies that Mickey had given her. She had been thinking of taking them home, but she decided to leave them in the office till the following day. She had been glancing at them all day and wondering what Mickey was trying to say to her: *I like you? I respect you? I pity you?*

The sun was still shining when she drove across the Ross Island Bridge. By the time she reached Southeast Boise, however, it had been covered by a thin gray veil of cloud, and the street looked strangely nostalgic, like a photograph from *Life* magazine, circa 1965. The apartment block in which the Beales lived was a two-story building made of cream-colored brick, with turquoise-painted shutters and a dead lime tree standing in front of it. A gang of kids were skateboarding along the sidewalk using a homemade ramp. In the driveway, a short, fat woman in a headscarf was washing what looked like a brand-new Malibu.

Holly parked and approached the woman washing her car. "Pardon me. I'm looking for Mrs. Hannah Beale."

The woman kept her back turned to her, so Holly couldn't see if she was answering. She walked around the car until she was facing her, and said, "I'm sorry— do you know where I can find Mrs. Hannah Beale?"

The woman looked Holly up and down. She was pale and puffy-faced, with eyes like raisins pushed into dough. She wore a bronze satin blouse and flappy white pants that were two inches too short for her, and strappy white sandals. A single hair grew from a mole on her chin and spiraled around.

"*I'm* Hannah Beale, for the second time. Who wants to know, for the second time?"

Holly produced her ID. Mrs. Beale peeled off one of her pink rubber gloves and examined it closely. "Children's Welfare Department? What's this?"

"The police department got in touch with us. . . . It's only a matter of routine."

"Jeez! I *told* those cops—how many times did I tell them?—Casper's sick. He has to have his chemo, even if he doesn't like it, or else he's going to die." Holly could detect an accent, northern Minnesota or maybe southeastern Manitoba, with a rise at the end of every sentence so that it came out like a question.

"We wanted to know if there was anything we could do to help," said Holly. "It can't be very easy for you, taking care of a child so sick."

"I'm fine. I can manage. Did somebody say I couldn't manage?"

"Is Casper your only child?"

Mrs. Beale jerked a thumb toward the skateboarders. "That's Thomas—the one in the green T-shirt—and Kyra; she's the girl in the pink." Holly shielded her eyes against the gray afternoon glare. Thomas and Kyra both looked like their mother, squat and overweight. Kyra was only about thirteen, Holly would have guessed, but her stomach bulged over her cherry-colored jogging pants as if she were five months' pregnant. Thomas had tight ginger curls and more ginger freckles than face.

"How about *Mr.* Beale?" asked Holly.

"*Daah,*" said Mrs. Beale disgustedly, flapping her glove.

"But you're managing okay?"

"I'm doing fine, thank you. I'm not saying it's easy."

She dropped her sponge into her foam-filled bucket and waddled over to the side of the apartment block to turn on the hose. Holly stood back while she sprayed the Malibu from front to back.

"Any chance I could see Casper?" asked Holly.

"For what?" asked Mrs. Beale. "He's been real sick today. He needs his sleep."

"Like I say, it's only routine."

"Well, there's no need. He was howling this morning because he doesn't like his treatment, that's all it was. It makes him nauseous, you know?"

"All the same, I'd still like to see him."

"I don't think so, miss. He's too sick to see people today."

Holly waited while Mrs. Beale polished her car with a chamois leather. "Can you tell me what hospital he's being treated at?"

No reply.

"Is it a local hospital? Providence St. Vincent, maybe?"

"What do you want to know that for?"

"It's just for my records."

"As if I don't get enough busybodies poking their noses into my private business."

"Well, I'm sorry, but Casper was screaming loud enough for somebody to call the police, and the Children's Welfare Department has a statutory obligation to follow it up."

Mrs. Beale stopped polishing and snapped the wet leather in the air. *Snap!* and *snap!* as if she were making a particularly vehement point about something. Her two children had stopped skateboarding and had come to join her, standing close to their mother with sullen, spoiled expressions on their faces. *God*, thought Holly. *Talk about the Addams Family.*

"Hi," Holly said brightly. "You're Kyra, aren't you? I love your barrettes." Your cheap, nasty, pink plastic hair slides.

Kyra wrinkled up her nose. "Who are *you*?"

"My name's Holly. I've come to see if your mom needs any help with your brother Casper."

"I'm managing *fine*, as a matter of fact," snapped Mrs. Beale impatiently. "If I needed any kind of damn help, I would've asked for it long since, wouldn't I?"

"That's terrific," said Holly. "So long as you're coping okay. Now, if I could just see Casper for a minute . . . It doesn't matter if he's sleeping."

"Well, I don't really think so," said Mrs. Beale. She pulled her children in closer to her side, and she shifted herself around so that she was standing in between Holly and the open door to the apartment block.

Holly hesitated. "Mrs Beale, if you won't let me see Casper today, I'll have to make arrangements to see him some other time."

"He's my son; he's sick but I take care of him good. I mean, what makes this any of your damned business?"

"I just need to make sure that he's receiving the best care possible, and that you're receiving all the help you're entitled to."

"You *talk* weird," sneered Thomas.

Holly smiled and pointed to her ear. "That's because I'm deaf. I haven't been able to hear anything since I was a little girl."

"You're *deaf?*" said Mrs. Beale in disbelief. She lifted up her eyes to appeal to the sky. "She's deaf, for Chrissakes, and she thinks she can bring up Casper better than me! Do you hear that, Thomas? They'll be sending around a cripple next, to teach you how to skateboard!"

"Mrs. Beale, you don't have to be so negative about this. I'm here to help you out, not to criticize you."

Mrs. Beale jabbed a finger at her. "I don't want none of your help. If it isn't bad enough, bringing up a child who won't be doing nothing in his life but dying. Now, you just get back in your vehicle and leave alone. I've got enough of a cross to bear without you climbing astride of it for the ride."

"I'm sorry," said Holly. "It wasn't my intention to upset you, but I'll have to see Casper sooner or later. If it's not convenient now, maybe you can tell me when."

"Are you going to leave me alone or what?"

"All right, I'll leave you alone."

"Then leave me alone. Get the hell out of here."

Holly shrugged, trying to look indifferent, even though her heart was beating twice as fast as normal. "I have to warn you, I'll be back, with a police officer if necessary."

Just as she was about to turn away, however, a small figure suddenly appeared in the doorway of the apartment block, like a ghostly apparition. It was a boy. A thin, chalk-white boy, wearing pale green pajamas. He was totally bald, and his face was shrunken in so that his eyes and his ears looked enormously out of proportion. He looked more like a sickly monkey than a human child. Holly was so shocked that she said "Oh my God" out loud.

"Momma!" the boy called out. His voice was surprisingly clear. "Momma, I've puked in my bed!"

Mrs. Beale glared at Holly and bustled up the drive. "How many times do I have to tell you not to come wandering outside? How many damn times?"

"But, Momma, I puked in my bed."

"Okay, okay, we'll get you cleaned up. Now, get back inside."

Holly skirted around the other two children and went right up to the doorway. The boy looked up at her with no curiosity at all. One leg of his pajamas was soaked in sour, milky vomit.

"Leave us alone," said Mrs. Beale. She spoke with her teeth clenched—*"Reave us arrone!"*—so that Holly could hardly understand her. "Can't you see how sick he is?"

"Of course I can see how sick he is. I can hardly believe that he isn't in a hospital."

"What? There's nothing that nobody can do for him in hospital."

"So who's his doctor?"

Mrs. Beale lifted Casper up in her arms. His wrists and his ankles were as thin as wooden spoons. "Keep your nose out, okay? *I'm* taking care of him. Nobody else can take care of him the way I can."

"Mrs. Beale, I'm going to come inside and I'm going to talk to Casper. I insist."

"Shove off, will you?"

"Mrs. Beale, you don't have any choice. If you try to stop me from talking to Casper, I *will* call the police."

Holly had to wait in the living room while Mrs. Beale changed Casper's pajamas. It was airless and stuffy and grotesquely overfurnished with Louis XIV-style armchairs and glass-topped wine tables and crushed-velour cushions. One side of the room was dominated by a forty-inch plasma-screen TV with a home movie center; the other by a glass-fronted liquor cabinet that was crowded with bottles of bourbon and brandy and amaretto. On the wall, in a lavish gilded frame, hung a blown-up color photograph of Mrs. Beale at Disneyland with Thomas and Kyra and Goofy. No sign of Casper.

Thomas and Kyra loitered in the living-room doorway, staring at Holly with those poisonous-pudding looks on their faces. It occurred to Holly that they probably weren't allowed into the room itself. There were too many breakable statuettes and fragile knickknacks and simulated-crystal souvenirs. On one table, on a little lace doily of its own, stood a snowstorm of Las Vegas, complete with Eiffel Tower.

Mrs. Beale reappeared carrying Casper in her arms. She propped him in one of the armchairs and sniffed her fingers. "Nothing worse than puke," she said.

She had knotted a red spotted scarf around Casper's head and changed him into faded red pajamas. He sat with his head resting against one of the cushions, staring at Holly unblinkingly. Holly shifted herself closer to him and took hold of one of his chilly little hands. He still smelled of vomit.

"Casper, my name's Holly. I've come by today to say hello and to make sure that you're okay."

"I'm okay," Casper whispered.

"I heard that you were kicking up kind of a fuss this morning."

"It was something and nothing," Mrs. Beale put in. "What do you expect when a kid's as sick as that? He doesn't understand that he has to get sicker to get better."

"I'm not going to get better," Casper said, and coughed.

"Of course you're going to get better," said Mrs. Beale. "Before you know it you'll be playing outside with Thomas and Kyra."

"I've heard you talking on the phone," Casper insisted.

"Casper, little boys who listen to other people's conversations will go to hell, I'm telling you that, as sure as eggs is chickens."

Casper rolled his eyes toward Holly and feebly

squeezed her hand. "I'm going to die," he assured her. He was so certain, so calm, that Holly felt a painful constriction in her throat. "I'm not scared. Sometimes I wish that I could go to sleep and never wake up."

Afterward, out on the porch, Holly said, "Mrs. Beale, you have to give me the name of Casper's doctor."

Mrs. Beale kept pulling at her gold chain necklaces, over and over, as if she were trying to saw her head off. "Dr. Ferdinand, that's his doctor."

"Dr. Ferdinand? Okay, where?"

"What do you mean, *where?*"

"I mean which clinic—which hospital?"

"East Portland Memorial, the children's cancer clinic."

"You have a number?"

"Go find it yourself. I have to go back to Casper."

"Okay, thanks for your help."

Mrs. Beale blinked at her aggressively. "What's that, 'Thanks for your help'? You trying to be smart or something?"

"I just said 'Thanks for your help.' You don't have to read anything into it."

Mrs. Beale started jabbing her finger again. "You listen to me: You're a deaf person. Don't you come round to my house trying to tell me how to take care of my kid. Don't you even think about it. If I hear that you've been harassing Dr. Ferdinand, you're going to regret it for the rest of your life. You got that?"

Holly stared at her for a long time, saying nothing. She was trying to look as if she couldn't be intimidated, no matter what, and that she intended to do whatever it took to check up on Casper's condition. But she could see that Mrs. Beale was unimpressed. In fact, she wasn't even interested. Her eyes were unfocused, as if she were thinking about something else altogether.

"Well, there's no doubt I'll see you again," said Holly, and Mrs. Beale immediately closed the door.

Holly was walking back to her car when a woman in ill-fitting high heels came tottering across the street toward her. She wore a yellow checkered dress and scarlet lipstick, and there was blobby mascara on her eyelashes. "How is he?" she flustered.

"Oh, you mean Casper? Not too good, I'm afraid."

"I feel *so* sorry for Hannah. What a terrible thing, to watch your child wasting away like that."

"Yes, it's tough." Holly unlocked her car and threw her briefcase onto the passenger seat.

"We were all hoping that we could give him one more vacation," the woman told her. "Do you think he's going to be well enough for that?"

"I don't know," said Holly. "I'm going to be talking to his doctor; he should be able to tell me." She paused, and then she said, "Who's 'we'?"

"The Casper Beale Cancer Fund. It's just me and six or seven neighbors, but we've managed to raise thousands. We sent him to Disneyland last October, and we've paid for all kinds of special treatments."

Holly frowned. Now that this woman came to mention it, she vaguely remembered reading something about The Casper Beale Cancer Fund in the *Portland Tribune*. There might have been an item on TV too.

"The last thing we bought was that car, so that Hannah could take him on outings and to the Tasco Clinic in Seattle. Twenty-one thousand dollars we raised for that."

"That's wonderful. Hannah's real lucky to have neighbors like you."

"Well, we're pretty damn proud of ourselves. That's what my husband likes to say. He was in the Navy."

"Mickey Slim"
Comes to Supper

When she parked in the alleyway beside Torrefazione, she was surprised to see Mickey's black Aurora parked there too. She climbed the stairs, and as she put her key in the lock she heard laughter from inside her apartment—Daisy's and Mickey's laughter—and the television playing. She walked in to find Daisy and Mickey on the couch together and Marcella in the kitchen chopping onions.

"Mommy!" said Daisy, jumping up. "Uncle Mickey's been helping me with my math homework! He showed me how to do multiplication! It's *easy!*"

Holly gave her a kiss but kept her eyes on Mickey. "It's *Uncle* Mickey now, is it? When did you marry my sister, Mickey, not that I have one?"

"Heeeyy . . . ," said Mickey, sprawling back on the couch. "I thought it sounded more family, you know?"

"I see." She took off her raincoat, hung it up, and propped her briefcase and her laptop on the chair by the kitchen door. "And to what do I owe the pleasure of this unexpected visit?"

"I can leave it till tomorrow if you like. I don't want to be a nuisance or nothing."

"You promised to stay for supper," said Daisy, jumping back onto the couch next to him. "Uncle Mickey *can* stay for supper, can't he, Mommy?"

"What is it you want, exactly?" Holly asked him. "It's been a long day, and I'm due in court first thing tomorrow."

"Hey," said Mickey, standing up. "I totally understand. I'm sorry. It was insensitive of me. I just thought that, since I was passing and there were one or two things I needed to talk to you about . . ."

"I'm sorry."

He peered at her bruise. "All the colors of the rainbow already. That's a sure sign that it's getting better."

She didn't say anything, but Mickey stayed where he was and didn't take his eyes off her. Then he said abruptly, "I'm out of here."

"No!" Daisy insisted. "You *have* to stay for supper. You *promised.*"

Mickey picked up his coat. "Sorry, spud. Your mom needs to rest. She needs to take a bath, close her eyes, and think about puppies and ponies and bright-colored candies. I'll come for supper some other night."

Holly hesitated for a moment. Then she went to the kitchen doorway and said, "Marcella, what are we having tonight?"

"*Peperonata con carne di maiale*—pork with peppers."

"You cooked enough for three?"

"Three? I cook enough for three hundred."

"In that case, Mickey, you're staying. Come on—it'll do me good."

"You're sure?"

She nodded. It *would* do her good. Being deaf, it was always easier to shut herself off from other people, especially when she felt distressed, but maybe she should take a few more risks. Maybe she should even risk Mickey's sympathy.

"Sounds great to me," grinned Mickey. "Look, I took the liberty of pouring myself a glass of your wine. Do you want some?"

"Yes, yes, thanks. Daisy, why don't you go help Marcella?"

"Oh, do I *have* to?" said Daisy.

"Please, pumpkin. Mommy has to talk to Uncle Mickey about work."

Mickey poured her a large long-stemmed glass of pinot noir. "You heard any more about Daniel Joseph?" he asked her.

"Still critical but stable. He's holding his own."

In the kitchen Marcella was noisily frying red and yellow peppers. Daisy came out with the knives and forks and set the table. Marcella put her head around the door and mimed, *Supper in two minutes, Ms. Summers!*

"Thanks, Marcella."

Mickey said, "The other thing is—the reason I came around here—we located Merlin Krauss. One of our guys recognized him yesterday afternoon in the Compass Hotel on the waterfront."

"That was good work."

"Well, yes and no. We still don't have any idea who

his hit man is, or who he's arranging to hit—if he's actually going to hit anybody—or on whose behalf he's going to hit her. But we do know that he's set up some kind of import-export business on Kearney, under the name of John Betchuvic."

"Coming to the table now!" called Marcella, and Holly waved back to show that she had understood.

Mickey leaned even closer. "So far as we can tell, Krauss isn't involved in drugs or gunrunning or anything serious like that, but he's running a couple of minor scams up and down the coast. Like, he's avoiding duty on imported sportswear by shipping the tops into Portland and the pants into San Diego. Separate tops and pants are no damn good to anybody, so he picks them up at U.S. Customs auctions for practically nothing. Then he matches them up again and sells them at premium prices. Illegal, but not exactly Al Capone."

"So what do you want me to do?"

"How do you know I want you to do anything?"

"Because you wouldn't have bothered to come around here otherwise. You would have sent me a text message."

"I came around because Daisy needed urgent help with her multiplication."

"No you didn't."

"All right, I came here to give you your birthday present. Sorry it's two days late."

He reached down beside the couch and produced a large box wrapped in shiny gold paper with a silver bow on it.

"Mickey, for goodness' sake. You didn't have to do that."

"Of course I did. I love you more than any child welfare officer I know. Go on, take it."

"Not until I know what you want me to do."

"You see right through me, don't you?"

"No, I can't. I can't see round corners."

"All right," he said. "Merlin Krauss does most of his business at the Compass, in the Sternwheeler Bar. I've been talking to the barman and Krauss kind of holds court there while various people come and go. I'd like to take you there tomorrow afternoon and see if you can pick up on anything he's saying."

"I have a welfare appointment in the Hawthorne District at three."

"Can't you put it off?"

"No, I can't. Supposing it turns out to be another Daniel Joseph?"

"Okay, Friday, then. How about Friday?"

The Beauty of the World

After supper, when Marcella had washed up the dishes and gone home, they sat in the living room together and finished the bottle of pinot noir. Daisy sat close to Mickey, and Holly could tell that she loved having a man in the house. David had been killed when Daisy was only three years old, and she could scarcely remember him, although she kept a faded color photograph of him next to her bed and she always talked to her friends about the times when "my daddy used to take me for long, long walks" and "my daddy always let me have as much candy as I wanted." Holly had never told her that the "long, long walks" had been a single stroll around Hoyt and Irving one August evening, and the candy had been a single bag of M&M's.

"Come on, Daisy, bedtime," Holly said at last.

"Can't I stay up late tonight?"

"You have school in the morning and I have to go to court."

"But Uncle Mickey's here."

Mickey said, "I'll tell you what: If you go to bed now,

I'll tell you a story. It's an old, old story that my mother used to tell me, and my grandmother used to tell my mother, and my great-grandmother told my grandmother. It's probably the oldest story in the world, except for the story I always tell when I'm late for duty."

Mickey sat on the edge of Daisy's bed while Holly had to share the pine rocking chair in the corner with about fifteen knobbly-kneed and sharp-elbowed Barbies. Holly was beginning to feel very tired, but she hadn't seen Daisy so happy for such a long time, and she managed to raise a smile. Daisy's eyes were shining in the light from her pink frilly bedside lamp.

Holly thought to herself: *I wonder if I could let another man into my life . . . just for Daisy's sake?*

Mickey said, "This is a story about a lonely king who was looking for a queen. The lonely king went riding in the forest one winter's day, *clippety-clop, clippety-clop*. The ground was covered in snow, and as he came to a clearing a raven came and perched on a hollybush next to him—*caw! caw!*—to peck at the bright red holly berries. The lonely king said, 'I am not going to rest until I find a queen who has hair as black as that raven's wing, and cheeks as white as the snow, and lips as red as those berries.'

"He went riding on a little further, *clippety-clop, clippety-clop*, and he came to a churchyard. Four men were sitting outside the churchyard with an open coffin in which a dead man was lying, with the snow falling on him. 'Why don't you bury him?' asked the lonely king, but the men said, '*Boo-hoo,* we don't have enough money for a funeral.'

"The lonely king said, 'He must be buried; it is only

right,' and he laid five gold coins on the dead man's chest and went riding off, *clippety-clop, clippety-clop*. He rode and he rode, and as night fell he realized he would have to find somewhere to stay for the night. After a while he saw somebody swinging a lantern in the darkness. It was a red-haired man all dressed in leather, with a sack on his back. He said, 'My lord, I know where you can rest your head this very night, and also find your heart's desire.'

"The lonely king invited the red-haired man to climb up on the back of his horse, and the red-haired man guided him to a tall, crumbling castle by the sea. They knocked on the door, *rappity-rap*, and they were answered by an elderly king with a long white beard, who invited them to stay for the night and to share some of his meat loaf.

"While the lonely king and the red-haired man were eating their meat loaf, a beautiful girl came tripping down the stairs, *trippity-trip*, with hair as black as a raven's wing, and cheeks as white as snow, and lips as red as holly berries. For the lonely king—*whoa!*—it was love at first sight.

"He asked the elderly king if he could take his daughter's hand in marriage. The elderly king agreed, but the daughter said, 'You shall not have me unless you keep safe this comb and give it back to me in the morning.' She gave the lonely king a silver comb and he put it in his pocket.

"When they were getting ready for bed, however, the red-haired man said, 'Do you still have the comb, master?' And when the lonely king searched in his pocket, he found that it was gone. He went to bed deeply upset, and wept so much that he soaked his pillow. I mean, some crybaby, or what?

"But the red-haired man opened up his bag, and out of his bag he took a dark cloak and some slippery shoes and a sword made of shining white light. He tippy-toed downstairs, and he saw the daughter leaving the castle with the silver comb in her hand. He followed her to the seashore, where she threw a seashell into the water—*splish!*—which magically became a boat. He did the same—*splish!*—and he rowed behind her to a rocky island.

"On the island, next to a flickering fire, sat a giant. The daughter gave him the silver comb and told him what she had done. 'Lock it in your treasure chest,' she said, 'and keep it safe for me.' The giant dropped the silver comb in his treasure chest, but the red-haired man fished it out again with the tip of his sword before the giant had time to lock it, and he rowed back to the mainland.

"In the morning the lonely king presented the daughter with the silver comb, and she was so furious that she made smash of every dish on the breakfast table—*smash! smash! smash!* She said, 'You shall not have me unless you keep safe these scissors and give them back to me in the morning.'

"Again that night the lonely king found that the scissors had disappeared out of his pocket. *Boo-hoo, boo-hoo*. But again the red-haired man put on his dark cloak and his slippery shoes and followed the daughter to the seashore, and rowed out to the island. He caught the scissors with the tip of his sword just as the giant tossed them into his treasure chest, and took them back to the lonely king. The next day the daughter was so angry that she smashed every dish on the breakfast table and all the chairs as well—*smash! crash! smash! crash!*—and threw a whole box of Cheerios out of the window.

"On the third day she said to the lonely king, 'Very well . . . I will marry you in the morning if you bring me the last lips I kiss tonight.' The lonely king thought that this was probably hopeless, but agreed to try. That night the red-haired man put on his dark cloak and his slippery shoes and followed her down to the seashore, and across to the giant's island. The daughter said to the giant, 'Kiss me, to make sure that your lips are the last lips I kiss tonight.'

"Once the daughter had rowed back to the mainland, the red-haired man took out his sword of white light and with one blow he cut off the giant's head—*whackkk!* He dropped the head in a sack and carried it back to the lonely king, who stored it under his bed.

"The next morning the daughter said, 'I don't suppose you have the last lips that I kissed last night.' But the lonely king tossed the giant's head onto the breakfast table and said, 'There they are, and weren't they ugly enough?' The daughter smashed every dish on the table—*smash! smash! smash!*—and threw a plateful of fried eggs and the cat out of the window. But she had given her word, and she had to marry him.

"The red-haired man said, 'Take her out, and strap her to two trees, and beat her with branches, because she has six devils in her.' And that is what he did, and when he beat her, great balls of fire came roaring out of her mouth. But when the fire was gone, she was the sweetest girl that you could ever have met; then he let her loose, and they were married.

"The lonely king said to the red-haired man, 'I must pay you for this.' But the red-haired man said, 'You already have. I was the man in the coffin, lying dead and unburied, and you paid for my funeral, and this was the only way I could thank you.' "

Daisy stared at Holly and said, "Wow. Seriously spooky."

Mickey's Gift

Later, in the living room, with her shoes off and her feet tucked under her, Holly said, "That was some story."

"That was the edited version. The way my grandmother told it, it went on all night, with giants jumping through prison bars and getting themselves cut in half, and mad goblins, and talking fish, and God knows what else."

"Daisy adored it. You're really good with her."

"I have a little girl of my own someplace. About a year older than Daisy."

"I didn't know that you and Sandy had a daughter."

"We didn't. She was somebody else's. That was the reason Sandy and me split up. Well, *one* of the reasons we split up."

"I'm sorry. Don't you ever get to see her? Your daughter, I mean?"

Mickey shook his head. "Her mother and I had what you might call a tempestuous relationship. Screaming, fighting, smashed dishes."

"Boxes of Cheerios out of the window?"

"Oh, yes. Cats and fried eggs too. In the end I thought it was better if I graciously bowed out."

"I didn't mean to pry."

"No, forget it. I don't think about it anymore."

"Ever thought of marrying again?"

"Got to find the right woman. Hair like a raven's wing, cheeks as white as snow, lips as red as holly berries. Here . . . ," he said, passing over the shiny gold box with the silver bow. "Why don't you open your birthday present?"

"All right," Holly said, and untied the ribbon. She carefully took off the paper, opened the box, and folded back the turquoise tissue paper. She lifted out a porcelain doll over fifteen inches tall, dressed like Cinderella in white lace and gold, with glass slippers and a sparkly tiara. The doll's face was almost ridiculously sweet, with heart-shaped, hand-painted lips and bright green eyes. "I'm stunned," said Holly, and she was.

"I hope it wasn't a stupid thing to buy you. It was just . . . well, I was stopped in traffic at the corner of Ninth and Multnomah and I saw it in KB's window. Staring at me. For some reason, I don't know, I just thought of you."

She shook her head and said, "It must have cost you a fortune."

"Police discount."

"She's beautiful. I don't know what to say." Nobody had given Holly a doll since she was seven years old. After she had lost her hearing, her relatives had always given her picture books for her birthday presents, and boxes of paints and raffia-weaving sets, as if she needed occupational therapy. As if she were no longer a pretty and playful young girl but a retard.

Mickey volunteered, "They had a Prince Charming doll, too, but he looked as if he batted for both sides."

"Daisy's going to be so jealous. Look, her glass slippers come off. And look at her tiny earrings!"

Mickey watched her with a lopsided smile. "Cinderella," he said. "Just like you. Frumpy welfare worker by day, ravishing princess by night."

Holly stopped tweaking Cinderella's bright blond hair. There was an expression in his eyes which she couldn't quite interpret. Amusement, partly. And flirtation too. But *calculation* as well—as if he were planning something mischievous that included her. "All you have to do is wave that magic wand," he told her.

"Yes . . . but what happens when the clock strikes twelve and I go back to being a frumpy welfare worker again?"

"You're still the same person, aren't you? Under the frump."

She laid Cinderella back in her box and folded the tissue paper over her.

Mickey sat forward. "You're not just pretending that you like it?"

"Of course not. She's wonderful."

"I kept the receipt."

"Don't be silly. I *love* her."

"I saw an apron and I nearly bought that. It had printed on the front: *You Ain't Heard Nothin' Yet.*"

She laughed and gave him a playful slap on the arm. She couldn't think of anybody else who would have had the nerve to say that to her. He snatched hold of her wrist and said, "Hey . . . I could arrest you for that. Assault and battery."

There was one of those moments when the clock hesitates, as if it can't decide if it ought to carry on ticking. Then he let go of her and reached for his wineglass. "Listen . . . I have to go. It's an early call in the morning."

At the front door he gently held her elbow and kissed her on the lips. "Thanks for this evening. Good food, beautiful family. What more could a guy ask for?"

"I'll see you in court tomorrow."

"Sure," he said, and went downstairs, raising one hand behind him in casual salute. Holly went back into her apartment and closed the door. She stood for a long time in the middle of the living room, her fingertips pressed against her mouth, wondering what she ought to be feeling.

Omen

She had a dark and knotty dream that night—a dream in which she was tangled up in nets and snares, and her struggles alerted the attention of something terrible. It lurched and fluttered unsteadily toward her: something black, something utterly inhuman, something that made the nets tremble and sway.

At seven-thirty the next morning, when she let up the primrose-yellow blind in her bedroom window, the sun was eating away at the upper slopes of Mount Hood. The mountain looked remote and enigmatic today, like the unfinished pyramid on the back of a dollar bill, and the sun looked like its mysterious shining eye.

She felt it was an omen. But an omen of *what*, she couldn't even begin to imagine.

Daisy sat in front of Holly's dressing-table mirror, screwing and unscrewing her lipsticks while Holly braided her hair.

"I *like* Uncle Mickey," Daisy declared. "Can he come around for supper again tonight?"

"I don't think so, pumpkin. He's very busy."

"But he said he'd tell me another story, about a mermaid. I liked the story about the lonely king and the dark
cloak and the slippery shoes. I wish *I* had slippery shoes."

"Well, if I see him today, I'll ask him."

"He has a cell phone. He gave me the number in
case I ever needed him."

Holly was having difficulty with Daisy's braids. For
some reason she couldn't remember whether it was right
over left or left over right. She had managed to plait only
about two or three inches and she simply couldn't do
more. It was like seeing a familiar face and completely
forgetting the person's name.

She tried again, but all she succeeded in doing was
tying Daisy's hair into a knot. She pulled it free and
Daisy squealed and said, *"Ow!* That hurt!"

"I'm sorry. . . . I think you'll just have to go to school
with ribbons in your hair."

"I don't want ribbons! I don't like ribbons: They're
babyish!"

"Listen, I don't have time to do your braids. I have
to be in court at eight-thirty."

"I'm not having ribbons!"

"All right, then, don't have ribbons! If you didn't
have your hair so long, you wouldn't have to tie it up at
all!"

"Barbie has long hair! Barbie always has long hair!"

Holly tossed the comb onto the kitchen table. *Screw
Barbie,* she thought. She felt so strange, so disoriented,
that she had to go through to the living room and stand
by the window and take deep, steadying breaths.

Object of Desire

The court buildings were crowded and noisy, with people rushing in all directions like an episode of *Hill Street Blues*. A senior official in Portland's planning department had been accused of accepting a 5-series BMW and a three-week vacation on Oahu from a wealthy local developer, and the marble hallways echoed with desperate questions from reporters and the clattering of feet.

Doug was waiting for Holly outside the juvenile division, along with a bespectacled young attorney with a Multnomah Bar Association necktie and a raging red zit on his nose.

"You know Ron Williams, don't you?" said Doug.

"Sure. How are you doing, Ron?"

"Fine, thanks. I don't think you're going to have any problems at all with this one. Dr. Sokol sent over all the necessary medical files and X-rays first thing this morning. And Judge Yelland is presiding. She doesn't believe that parents should even *frown* at their children, let alone jump on them."

"What time are we scheduled for?"

"There's only two more applications before ours. The Thompson case could go on a while; kid had his head squeezed in a workshop vise, but the father says it was a party game that went wrong. You know the game: You crush some kid's head flat and then everybody else has to guess who they are." He sniffed and checked his watch. "Say, forty-five minutes."

"Okay, I think I'll go find myself a coffee."

As she was going back down to the lobby, she met George Greyeyes coming up. "George . . . I didn't know you were going to be here."

George was wearing a smart navy blazer and smelled of Tommy Hilfiger. "I want to keep an eye on this one, that's all. I don't want National Indian Child Welfare Association looking negligent in any respect . . . nor the Children's Welfare Department, either."

"George, this is only going to be a formality."

"Sure. But you know me: I don't like surprises. The last time the Indians took the white men at their word, they lost ninety percent of Oregon."

They went downstairs to the coffee shop and took a table in the corner. On the other side of the room, four young lawyers and a woman paralegal were huddled over a heap of papers, obviously trying to hammer out a divorce settlement before their case came up in front of a judge.

"—maybe we can cut you some slack on the marital home. Maybe sixty-five, thirty-five. But that's as far as we can go."

"What about the cabin?"

"Same deal."

"My client won't accept that. She wants the cabin one hundred percent. What does he think he's going to do, *time-share?*"

George said, "We need to learn some lessons from this Daniel business. Maybe we need to set up a regular interface between your people and my people, so that we can share any kind of suspicion about a child at risk, any kind of gut feeling, whether it's medical or cultural, whether it's substantiated by prima facie evidence or not. I mean, let's get in there *before* it happens, not after."

Holly said, "Sure." She was interested in what George had to say, but she knew that it would do very little good. All the interfaces in the world would never stop a parent from staggering home, drunk or high or simply angry, and thrashing a defenseless child. For some reason she couldn't take her attention away from the conversation on the other side of the coffee shop.

One of the lawyers was saying, "It's seriously going to disorient the kids, isn't it, if they spend the first week in August with mom and her partner and then the second week in August with dad and whatever bit of fancy goods dad has decided to bring along with him, both in the same vacation environment? I mean, we're not just talking moral values here; we're talking bedroom farce."

"Then maybe they should sell the cabin and split the proceeds."

"No way. That cabin is an integral part of the children's recreational life. My client thinks that they've lost enough already, losing their father. She doesn't want to stunt their emotional development too."

"Jesus. I didn't even have a treehouse when I was a kid, and do I look stunted?"

Two of the lawyers and the paralegal stood up and left the coffee shop, obviously off to consult with their client. The two remaining lawyers sprawled at their table, one of them breaking the corners off cookies and nibbling them like a chipmunk.

George said, "It isn't easy for me to explain how important the spirits still are to most Native Americans. Spirits of water, spirits of wind, spirits of rocks and trees. In some ways they're more important than they ever were, because they're the only link we have left with the people we once used to be, and the country that once used to be ours."

One of the lawyers nudged his friend. "That Indian guy, do you know him?"

"I've seen him a couple of times. Big Chief In-Tray, from the Native American Children's Society, or something like that. Looks like a noble savage, but he's an *i*-dotter and a *t*-crosser."

"How about the tail?"

"Yeah . . . I was checking her out. I think she works for Children's Welfare. Great gazongas. That really lights my fire, you know: a tailored suit and great gazongas. Nice legs too. Seriously nice legs."

"Hey . . . what do you think? She'd be great for one of the old man's parties, wouldn't she? I mean, take a look at those lips. She looks like she's permanently puckering up to give you a blow job."

"*Her?* Are you shitting me?"

"No, it'd be a real challenge, wouldn't it, someone like that?"

The second lawyer grinned in disbelief and shook his head.

"No, I mean it. What a challenge. I'll tell you what I'm going to do: I'm going to find out who she is. I mean, that would be a gas, wouldn't it? A Children's Welfare officer for one of the old man's parties?"

George touched her arm. "Holly . . . Holly, you're not listening to me."

"Sorry, George. Guess I got a little distracted."

"Lipreading again? Remember it's a gift, Holly. Not a right."

"I know, George. Sorry. What were you saying about this interface?"

While George went to the bathroom, Holly made a performance of leafing through her court papers, but every now and then she glanced across at the two lawyers to try to work out what they were saying. She had often picked up compliments before, and sometimes she had picked up crude remarks about her figure, and once she had lip-read an assistant district attorney calling her "a goddamned nit-picking nuisance with an ego as big as her tits," but what did these two mean when they talked about "a challenge"? And what were "the old man's parties"?

The cookie-nibbling lawyer said emphatically, "I can ask. If not, —— will know who she is." He was swallowing at the time, and Holly couldn't quite catch the name.

"Yeah, you're right," agreed the other one. "He works with Children's Welfare, doesn't he?"

The cookie-nibbler nodded a few times and then started talking about his new Cadillac Escalade.

George came back, smelling of industrial soap. "Are you all right?" he asked her.

"Why? Why shouldn't I be?"

"You look like your cat just died."

"Do I? I don't have a cat." She tidied up her papers. Then she said, "If I said 'the old man's parties,' would that mean anything to you?"

George looked blank. "'The old man's parties'? Is this a riddle?"

"I don't know. I don't know what it means. I get the feeling that it's something unpleasant, that's all."

Doug came down at 10:25 to tell them that the Joseph application was on. They followed him out of the coffee shop, and as they left, the two lawyers swiveled around in their chairs to watch her. She turned and one of them winked at her, while the other one said, "Classy ass, too, I'm telling you."

The Curse of Raven

The hearing took less than four minutes. Silver-haired and sharply pointed of nose, Judge Imogene Yelland immediately granted the application for Daniel Joseph to be made a ward of the court pending the prosecution of Elliot Joseph for child abuse and a full welfare report and psychiatric report on Mary Joseph.

Mary Joseph's attorney rose to protest that nobody had yet been convicted for beating up on Daniel, and that there was no proof that Mary Joseph was a neglectful mother. "Accidents do happen in the home, and there are plenty of recorded instances in which parents have been erroneously blamed for childhood injuries."

Judge Yelland stared at him as if he had exposed himself. "I hope you're not trying to suggest that Daniel Joseph's injuries were in any respect *self-inflicted*, Mr. Leiderman?"

"I, ah—"

"Mr. Leiderman, if you are capable of pulling your pants down around your ankles and jumping on your own pelvis seven times, it would be most educational to see you do it."

Nobody laughed. Mary Joseph's attorney reddened and sat down.

"Next application," said the clerk. George turned to Holly and blew out his cheeks in relief. Judge Yelland had made no comments about the failure of the National Indian Child Welfare Association or the Portland Children's Welfare Department to foresee what had happened. All the same, that could well come later, when Elliot Joseph came up for trial.

"I'll catch you in a minute," Holly mouthed, and patted George's shoulder. She left the juvenile division and walked across the echoing marble floor to the main court buildings. She found Detective Farrant outside Court Number 3, reading the sports pages and chewing gum with his mouth wide open.

"Mickey around?" she asked him.

He jerked his head toward the huge maplewood doors. "He just went in for the Joseph indictment. By the way, what did you *do* to him last night?"

"Me? Why?"

"The guy was like walking on air this morning. He actually bought me a doughnut."

"He came around to my place for dinner, that's all. Maybe I reminded him what it's like to be a normal human being."

"Mickey? I doubt it."

An usher opened the door of Court Number 3 for her, and she slipped into one of the seats at the back. Mickey was sitting behind the assistant district attorney and doodling on his notepad while Elliot Joseph's court-appointed lawyer made a windy application for bail.

"This man has been the victim since childhood of relentless discrimination and pernicious ethnic prejudice that would have broken anybody's spirit. Day after day, week after week, year after year, he was treated as a misfit and an outcast in the land which once used to belong to his natural ancestors. Is it any surprise that he was brought to the point of madness—a point where he lashed out blindly at what he had understandably grown to believe was an evil spirit that had made his entire life purposeless and utterly miserable, and now seemed to be threatening to do the same to his only son?"

As Holly made her way to the front of the court, Elliot Joseph turned his head around to see who it was. He was wearing bright orange prison coveralls. His greasy gray hair was sticking up wildly, both of his eyes looked like split-open eggplants, and his mouth was puffed up. All the same, he managed a grotesque grin and stared at her all the way to her seat.

"How's it going?" Mickey mouthed as she sat down beside him.

"Fine. Judge Yelland made the welfare order."

"Any news about the kid?"

"Critical but reasonably stable. They're worried about his left eye, though. Detached retina."

"I should have hit that bastard harder."

Holly glanced across at Mickey's notepad. He had sketched a mountain with thunderclouds around it, and dozens of pine trees with little stick people running around them.

"What's that?"

He flipped the notepad face down, as if he were embarrassed by it. "Nothing. Just dreaming of a little R & R."

"I'll catch up with you tomorrow afternoon," she said. "What time do you want me down at the Compass?"

"Make it three-thirty if you can. I'll meet you outside, in my car."

Elliot Joseph's lawyer finished making his application for bail and sat down. The presiding judge, Walter Boynton, was a mild, sniffy man with huge ears and white hair. He reminded her of Ray Walston, the TV actor who used to star in *My Favorite Martian*. He blew his nose with a large white handkerchief and made a long job of wiping it from side to side. Then he said, "Bail denied. The defendant will be kept in custody in the North County Correctional Facility until such time as a trial date can be arranged."

Holly looked over at Elliot Joseph. He was saying something, but because his lips were so swollen, it was very difficult for her to tell what it was. But there was no doubt that he was saying it to *her*. He was staring directly at her and he was rhythmically jerking his head in her direction to emphasize what he was saying.

"—*make sure it comes after you—however fast you run, you deaf bitch, wherever you hide—it's going to come after you—and it's going to tear you into pieces, I swear it on my boy's life—*"

Holly raised her hand against her face so that she couldn't see him. "Something wrong?" said Mickey.

"No. . . . I think this whole Daniel Joseph case has upset me, that's all."

He took hold of her hand and gave it a consoling squeeze. "Don't you worry. You think *I* was hard on that scumbag? You wait till he gets into jail. The cons have a special welcome for guys who beat up on little kids. A live-rat enema. A *hungry* live-rat enema."

"*Mickey—*"

"Sorry, sorry. Look, I'll see you tomorrow."

As Holly left the courtroom, Elliot Joseph was shuffling in his shackles back to the cells. She glanced back at him only once, but before he was jostled through the door she could see that he was mouthing the single word *Raven* at her, over and over. *Raven . . . Raven . . . Raven . . .* and with every *Raven* he was shaking his head at her in the way that a shaman shakes his medicine stick.

The Various Shapes of Fear

Holly and George rode a streetcar back to their offices. It was so crowded that they had to stand in the aisle, hanging onto the straps, and Holly was almost suffocated by a man standing next to her in a woolly bobble hat and a huge blue puffa jacket. The morning was so gloomy that it was difficult to believe it wasn't even 11:30 yet. The temperature had dropped, too, like a stone down a well. George said, "Feels like the end of the world, doesn't it?"

Holly said, "Tell me about Raven."

"*Raven?* Any particular reason?"

"I'm trying to understand why Elliot did what he did."

George shrugged. "Well, if he *did* think that Daniel was possessed by Raven, he would have blamed the poor kid for everything that went wrong in his life. Like I said, Raven is a scavenger who takes away people's luck. He takes it piece by piece. First your livelihood, then your home, then your loved ones, and last of all your happiness. Then, when you don't have any luck left, he takes *you*, and rips you apart, and feeds off your utter hopelessness.

"There are dozens of stories about Raven—hundreds—but in every one it's human misery that gets his juices flowing."

"You said he takes different shapes."

"That's right." George ducked his head so that he could see where they were. "He usually looks like a big black bird. Sometimes he doesn't have a beak, because there's some story about him turning into a man and trying to steal a fish from some fishermen, only the fishermen were too strong for him and pulled his jaw off. But most times he appears as someone you know . . . even someone you really like. Other times he's nothing but a shadow, or a cat, or a dog. Or even something inanimate, like a chair."

"Can anybody send him after you? I mean, if somebody really didn't like you and they wanted you to lose all of your luck, could they ask Raven to do that?"

George smiled. "That's a strange question."

"I'm interested, that's all."

"You got anybody specific in mind? Not that Lutz guy you were telling me about, the one in Accounts? The guy who keeps coming up to you at the watercooler and breathing onion-ring breath all over you?"

Holly gave him a wan smile. "Oh, no. I wasn't thinking of trying it myself. I just wondered if that was part of the legend . . . you know, that somebody could send Raven looking for somebody else, to get their revenge or something?"

"This is my stop. I can talk to you later if you like."

"No, I'll come with you. I can walk the rest of the way."

They stepped down from the streetcar, which rang its bell, closed its double doors, and hummed off north-ward toward the Pearl District, although to Holly it glided away in utter silence. The wind was growing blustery, so that the signs outside the coffeehouses and bookstores started to swing, and Holly had to tug down her black beret and button her long black trench coat up to the neck.

George linked arms with her. "So far as I know, the only time that you can ask Raven to do you a favor is if you see through one of his disguises and catch him be-fore he can change back into a bird and fly away."

"Like Elliot Joseph did with Daniel?"

"That's right."

"So Elliot Joseph could send Raven looking for one of us?"

"According to the legends, yes. But— Hey, what is this? It's only a story."

Holly stopped. On the opposite side of the street, parked outside the Bellman Bookstore, was a silver Porsche Spyder with its convertible top down. She stared at it for so long that George nudged her arm.

"What's the matter? I've been trying to talk to you and you haven't been looking."

"I'm sorry. It's nothing. I'm sorry. Look, why don't we meet up tomorrow morning and talk about this in-terface idea?"

"Okay . . . I'll check my diary and give you a call. You take care of yourself; you look like you could use a strong cup of coffee."

Holly stood on tiptoe and kissed his cheek. "Talk to you later, okay?" George disappeared through the reflecting glass doors of his office building, almost like a stage magician, but Holly stayed where she was, still staring at the Porsche. It was the same model, same year, same color, that James Dean had been driving when he was killed in California in 1955. James Dean had been David's hero, and David had owned a Porsche almost exactly like it. And died in it too.

Now here it was, parked on Salmon Street, outside David's favorite bookstore, as if all the pages of the calendar had flurried back six and a half years, and David was still alive and still inside the store, browsing through the movie section.

Don't Look Behind You

She crossed the street and peered in through the bookstore window, shading her eyes with her hand, but it was too dark inside for her to be able to make out anything but occasionally shifting shadows. She turned back to the car. Seeing it parked there made her feel as if she had stepped up to her neck in icy-cold water. Only ninety models had been made, and of those only seventy-eight had been sold to the public, so the odds were that this was actually David's car, repaired and re-sprayed. A large cellophane-wrapped bouquet of yellow roses lay on the backseat.

She had hated this car. David had bought it out of a legacy from his aunt from Forest Grove. They could have used the money for a house, but when David heard the Porsche was up for auction he immediately put in a bid for it. He drove everywhere with the engine bellowing and the tires screaming like the Hallelujah Chorus. "You know, Jimmy said there were only two speeds in the Little Bastard: dead stop and *banzai!*" The way David used to talk about "Jimmy," you would have thought that James Dean had been his lifelong buddy.

Holly had agreed to take a ride in the Porsche only once. Even when she first climbed into it she felt as if she were sitting in her own coffin. David had grinned at her. He hadn't realized that he was sitting in his.

She hesitated briefly, and then she pushed open the door of the bookstore and stepped inside. She still couldn't catch her breath. The store was lined from floor to ceiling with secondhand books on every subject from fly-fishing to feng shui, and stacks of old magazines like *Life* and *The Saturday Evening Post*. The only light came from a row of windows at the rear of the shop, which were glazed with amber and yellow orchids.

There was the *smell*, too, of thousands of books whose former owners had no longer wanted. A sour and unhealthy smell, like that of a dayroom in a retirement home.

Holly walked cautiously along one of the aisles. A tall young man was standing at the very end, reading. He was silhouetted against the windows, so it was impossible for her to make out his face. But he was wearing a dark green Burberry, like David's, and his fringe brushed forward the way that David's had been. And as she came closer, she could see that he was standing in front of the movie section.

She had seen David dead. She knew beyond any question at all that he was dead. Yet, why was she walking toward this man half-expecting him to be David, returned from the grave as if he hadn't driven under a flatbed trailer at more than seventy miles per hour?

She remembered him lying in his white silk-lined casket, his shirt collar fastened up much higher than he normally wore it because his head had been ripped off. The mortician said it was a blessing that he had looked away at the very last second before impact because otherwise they would have had to opt for a closed casket.

Holly came closer to the man and stood looking at him from only three feet away. She still couldn't be sure if he was David or not. But then the sun began to come out, and the light in the amber-and-yellow windows gradually grew brighter, and the man became aware that she was looking at him.

"Can I help you?" he said, and of course he wasn't David at all. He had shaving-brush eyebrows and close-set eyes and a little clipped mustache.

"I, uh—I was trying to find a book on James Dean."

"I'm sorry, I don't work here. Maybe you should ask at the desk."

"Oh. Yes. Sorry."

He went back to his reading but Holly stayed close beside him. Eventually he looked up again and said, "The *desk*. It's right by the front door."

"Yes, I'm sorry. But do you mind if I ask you something?"

"Okay," he said suspiciously.

"That Porsche parked outside—is that yours?"

"Porsche? I don't even own a car. I'm a dedicated cyclist."

"Oh. Okay, sorry. I'll, uh, go to the desk."

"Okay."

A big bespectacled woman was sitting at the cluttered counter, sticking discounted price labels into a stack of encyclopedias. She wore a hand-knitted sweater in browns and purples, and her hair looked as if somebody had killed a struggling raccoon with knitting needles.

"Are you interested in something in particular, dear?" she asked. Holly could immediately detect that her accent wasn't Portland, more like Maryland or northern Virginia. It was the prissy, mannered way she said *pahtickle-uh.*

"No, sorry. I wasn't looking for a book. I thought I saw someone I knew."

The woman took off her spectacles and frowned at her. "Are you all *right?*" she asked.

"I'm fine. . . . It's just that I saw that Porsche parked outside and it's kind of a rare car and someone I knew used to own one."

The woman looked toward the door. The Porsche was gone. The only sign that it had been there at all was a dry rectangle on the street with streaks of rain running across it.

"Something's concerning you, isn't it, dear?" the woman said. "My nose always tells me when folks are feeling disquieted," and she tapped it by way of emphasis.

"I've had a difficult morning, that's all."

"You're not alone, though. You do realize that?"

"What do you mean?"

"I mean exactly that. You're not alone. There's something following you, dear. Something behind you."

Holly glanced around, but the woman touched her hand and said, "Don't do that. The thing that's following you, it's bad fortune, and you never want to turn around and look bad fortune in the eye—never."

"I really don't know what you're talking about."

"You don't? I think that maybe you do. I come from a long line of mothers and daughters who could tell when trouble was afoot. There's blood on the moon, that's what my mother used to say. And I can see that with you. I can see that as surely as if a black shadow was standing close behind you."

"Well, thank you for that," said Holly, more sharply than she had meant to. "Next time I'm feeling too cheerful, I'll know where to come."

"I'm only saying what I see, dear. I'm only telling you what my nose tells me."

The woman shrugged and placidly went back to her price labels. Holly stayed and watched her for a few moments. She was irritated by the woman's impertinence, but at the same time she was anxious to find out what she meant by *bad fortune*. What had George said about Raven? *Raven is a scavenger who takes away people's luck, bit by bit.*

After a while the man with the shaving-brush eyebrows came up to the desk carrying two books about George Stevens and David O. Selznick. He gave her a wary look and so she turned and left.

As she reached the door the woman looked up and said, "You remember what I said, dear: Don't you go looking behind you, whatever you do."

Blood on the Moon and
Other Expressions

On the second occasion that the Portland Police Bureau had asked her to help them to lip-read a surveillance video, one of the suspects had used the phrase *I wouldn't know him from Adam's housecat*.

Holly's interest had been aroused, because she had only ever heard anybody say *I wouldn't know him from Adam*. She had mentioned it to Dick Cass, a young English teacher she knew, and Dick had looked it up in the University of Portland library. It turned out that *Adam's housecat* was commonly used in southern states, while west of the Appalachians the saying changed into *I wouldn't know him from Adam's off-ox*.

She realized then that she could not only identify people's regional origins from their accents but from the names they called everyday things, from old cars to rocking chairs to fried potatoes. In West Virginia they called a clap of thunder *the old bread wagon* because rain made the crops grow. In Oregon they used the phrase *couple-three* to mean *several*.

Across the country she discovered that there were more than 176 different names for dust balls under the bed.

Some of the sayings were so locally specific that she could occasionally tell which county or even which town a suspect had been raised in. Pennsylvanians from the Manheim area still said that they "spritzed" the lawn instead of sprinkled it. When Texans from Brownsville complained that somebody was "admiring" them, they meant that they were being given the evil eye.

Down in certain parishes in Florida, people spoke of a place being "creepified" instead of scary. "That was a right boogerish place, that old house, real creepified."

Holly had been right to guess that the woman in the bookstore came from Maryland or northern Virginia. *Blood on the moon* was a Baltimore expression meaning a suspicious, menacing, or foreboding set of events.

A Black Painting

On an impulse she called Katie at the office and told her she was going to be half an hour late. She walked instead to Yamhill Street and went into the small, white-fronted Summers Gallery, which was owned and run by her older brother Tyrone. It was fashionably minimalist: The only painting displayed in the window was a naked man rendered in bright aqua-marine, entitled *Blue Roger.*

Inside, the gallery was cool and cream, with paintings spaced at tasteful intervals along the walls and several bronze and stone sculptures on stark white plinths. Tyrone was sitting at his desk at the rear of the gallery, talking on the phone. Apart from his phone/fax and the latest issue of *Architectural Digest,* there was nothing on his desk but a single yellow rose in a clear glass vase. A young man with scraggly bleached-blond hair and a faded denim jacket was sprawled on a tan leather armchair, idly tearing up a catalog of early American art, rolling it into little balls, and trying to toss them into Tyrone's discarded moccasins.

Tyrone himself looked strikingly like Holly, only very much taller. His hair was darker than hers, and his eyes were brown where hers were greenish-onyx. His nose was larger and sharper, but he had the same slightly fey quality, as if both of them might have been changelings. It was a look they had inherited from their Finnish forebears by way of their mother.

"Hi, Matthew," said Holly, to the paper-tosser. "You're not bored, by any chance?"

"Bored? Bored doesn't even come *close*. I am way beyond boredom, in a fourth dimension of total yawnation, where I am losing interest even in *breathing*."

Tyrone gave Holly a finger wave and said, "Sorry, Holly, I won't be long. I'm trying to arrange a special exhibition."

He listened, and nodded, and then he said, "Tsimshian transformation masks. Very deep Native American stuff. Like, very, *very* deep." Then, into the phone: "Yes, Ms. Spring Moon, I *do* understand their mystical significance. Yes, I know. Of course your shaman can supervise their hanging. We wouldn't want to upset any malevolent spirits, now, would we?"

As Tyrone talked, Matthew was mimicking his exaggerated hand gestures, so Tyrone threw the copy of *Architectural Digest* at him and hit him on the shoulder.

"*Ow!*" Matthew protested.

"I don't know why you don't find yourself something more challenging to do," Holly suggested, taking off her raincoat and sitting down next to him.

"I don't think there's anything more challenging in the whole world than trying to bug Tyrone. Except—I don't know—maybe climbing the east face of Mount Hood in midwinter, totally naked."

"Oh my God. So long as you don't expect me to watch you do it."

Holly waited for a while, but Matthew kept on tossing paper and Tyrone kept on talking, and nodding, and saying "Uh-huh, uh-huh," so in the end she stood up and walked along the gallery looking at the paintings. Most of them were strong, simplistic images in primary colors: nudes, abstracts, landscapes. But at the very end of the gallery there was a large painting propped up against the wall that appeared to be nothing but solid black.

When she approached it, however, she realized that the paint had varying textures, some of them glossy and some of them matte. In the very center, too, almost invisible from a distance, were two dark red circles, like totally bloodshot eyes. Viewing the painting from an angle, so that the lights shone across it, Holly was sure that she could distinguish the ragged outline of black feathers.

She suddenly felt as if somebody had come very close up behind her and was breathing against her neck. Her first instinct was to turn around, but then she thought of what the woman in the Bellman Bookstore had warned: *There's something following you . . . Something behind you : . . Don't you go looking behind you, whatever you do.*

This is completely irrational, she thought. *There can't be anybody there.* But she felt ridiculously reluctant to look around, and she was sure that somebody was breathing very close to her ear.

She was still standing in front of the black painting when Tyrone came up to her and put his arm around her shoulders. "What do you think of it?" he asked.

"I don't know. Who painted it?"

"Some guy who came in this morning. He asked if I'd consider selling it for him."

"Does it have a title?"

"It's called *Ill Fortune VII*. Don't ask me why. I haven't seen *Ill Fortune I* through *VI*."

"You're kidding me. That's what it's called?"

"Why should I kid you?"

"I don't know. I think I'm being, what, hypersensitive. Superstitious, maybe. It's just that somebody wished bad luck on me this morning and ever since then I keep on seeing things. I don't exactly know what you'd call them . . . *omens, I* guess."

"Omens? What? You mean like black cats and funeral processions and haloes around the sun?"

"No, I just mean things that make me feel uneasy." She told him how Elliot Joseph had put a curse on her in the courtroom, and about the Porsche parked on Salmon Street and what the woman in the Bellman Bookstore had said. "And now this painting, *Ill Fortune VII*. And it *could* be a raven, couldn't it?"

Matthew had joined them. He tilted his head on one side and said, "It could be a raven, yes. But then it could equally be the inside of Mike Tyson's shorts at midnight."

"For Christ's sake, Matthew," said Tyrone. Then to Holly: "Why don't you join us for lunch? We were only going across to the Quarter Deck for a sandwich."

Memories of Bad Luck

"Ever since you were a kid, you always seemed to know when bad things were going to happen, didn't you?" said Tyrone. He had put his half-glasses on and he was picking stray alfalfa sprouts off his plate and nibbling them. "Don't you remember that Fourth of July when that girl from next door got burned? What was her name?"

"Margaret Pickard," said Holly. "How could I ever forget?"

"What was that all about?" asked Matthew, his mouth obscenely full of sandwich.

Tyrone tidily patted his lips with his napkin. "I guess it was Holly's deafness: It gave her kind of a psychic awareness. You know, things that most people don't usually pick up on. She could always tell you if it was going to rain, for instance."

"In Portland? You don't need a psychic awareness for that. It happens once every fifteen minutes, without fail."

"No, there were other things too. Like, she could tell

when the phone was going to ring about ten seconds before it did. And once we were walking through Waterfront Park and an old guy was mowing the grass on a ride-on mower and Holly said, 'You have to stop him, he's going to hurt himself.' Well, our dad went over and talked to the old guy, but of course the old guy just laughed. The next thing we knew, he was trying to clear a piece of broken branch out of the mower blades, and somehow it started up and chopped most of his fingers off. I'll never forget that. He was standing there with his hand held up and only his thumb and half of his index finger left, and blood running off his elbow, and he was staring at Holly with this *look*, like she had actually made it happen."

"Excuse me. I'm trying to eat a very rare steak sandwich here."

"Well, come on, Matthew, you wanted to know. What happened on the Fourth of July was different, though. This girl next door, Margaret, she was only about eleven, and she was real quiet and never said a word to anyone. The neighbors had a big Fourth of July barbecue with a bonfire and professional fireworks. But Margaret's parents kept teasing her to mingle with the boys, and in the end she went off up to her room because she was so shy."

Holly said, "I was sitting in the garden, on a bench under the trees, and I had a premonition. I mean an actual *vision*, almost, of a girl falling, her arms spread out wide, and she was burning. It was, like, I don't know: like an angel falling out of heaven. You know those medieval paintings. The trouble was, I didn't know who it could be. I just kept on seeing it again and again."

"Holly came and told me," Tyrone put in. "I told my mom but my mom didn't really know what to do. It's a bit of a downer if you go up to your hosts at a Fourth of July party and say, 'Excuse me, my daughter's had this premonition that somebody's going to burn to death.' So mom told dad and between them they agreed to keep a careful eye on all of the kids around the bonfire."

"Right near the end of the party they had this incredible rocket display," said Holly. "There were dozens and dozens of rockets, and I saw Margaret come out onto the balcony in front of her parents' bedroom to watch it. I'll never forget it. She was wearing this white flouncy frock with a big pink bow, and a bow in her hair."

Tyrone said, "Something went wrong. One of the rockets misfired and flew toward the house. It hit Margaret and it exploded, and there was this terrible crackling noise—you know, like rockets make when they explode in the sky."

Holly shook her head, because of course she hadn't heard it herself. "Margaret caught fire. I could see that she was screaming. She spread her arms wide and she jumped off the balcony, and she fell onto the steps at the back of the house. They threw buckets of water over her and tried to roll her in a tablecloth, but the rocket was all magnesium and she kept on burning and burning and they couldn't put her out."

"Holy shit," said Matthew, putting down his sandwich and wiping his hands on his pants. "And you really *knew* that was going to happen?"

"I don't know. Maybe it was more of an intuition

than a genuine vision. After all, children *do* get burned at fireworks parties, don't they? Just like gardeners accidentally chop their fingers off in mowing machines."

Tyrone took hold of Holly's hand. "You're not feeling any bad vibes like that now, are you? Don't let this Joseph asshole get to you. He was the one who beat up on his kid, wasn't he? So you shouldn't let *him* make *you* feel guilty."

"I still feel—I don't know—maybe that woman in the bookstore was right. Maybe she could sense bad luck coming, the way I used to."

"Holly, there's no such creature as Raven. There's nothing after you. And if that painting really gives you the heebie-jeebies, I'll tell that guy to come and take it away."

"No, that's okay. It's only a painting, and like Matthew said, it's probably not a raven at all."

"You should take Katie and Doug up on their offer. Go off to the lake for the weekend, take a break. You deserve it."

"Maybe you're right."

"Hey, listen, Holly," said Matthew, "before you go, you don't see any bad luck coming *my* way, do you? I mean, if I'm going to catch fire or chop all my fingers off, I'd really like to know about it."

Tyrone rolled up his eyes in exasperation, but Holly said, "Okay, then, give me your hand." Matthew wiped it on his pants again and held it out. Holly held it for a while and closed her eyes.

"Yes. . . ." She nodded. "You're finally going to decide that bugging Tyrone *isn't* enough of a challenge."

"And?"

"Like you said, you're going to climb the east face of Mount Hood in midwinter, totally naked."

"Hey, I don't call that bad luck. That'll be cool!"

"Cool? You think so? You're going to run out of rations on the way up, and by the time you get to the top you're going to have nothing left but a frozen Twinkie."

Matthew tugged his hand away and gave her a playful slap. "Your sister, Tyrone! What a saucy mare!"

Blood in the Street

Holly and Tyrone left the Quarter Deck hand in hand while Matthew trucked along the sidewalk a few paces in front of them, snapping his fingers.

"What *do* you see in him?" asked Holly.

Tyrone smiled. "He keeps my feet on the ground. Stops me from being too queeny."

"You were never *queeny*. Just artistic."

"Holly, I know my weaknesses."

Holly said, "Katie and Doug are trying to pair me off with Katie's cousin. Some guy called Ned."

"You don't sound very enthusiastic about it."

"I don't know. I just don't like blind dates, that's all."

"It won't be a blind date; it'll be a deaf date."

She gave him two sharp nudges with her elbow, and he laughed and almost lost his balance on the curb.

"Sorry, sorry, sorry!" he said. "But seriously, I think it's about time you found somebody. It doesn't have to be the love of your life, after all. But you've always said that being deaf makes it difficult for you to socialize.

It's bound to. Why not give him a try? I mean, he can't be that much of a freak, can he?"

"You want to bet? He's in wood pulp."

"Oh. I have to confess that I don't know a whole lot about wood pulp."

"Neither do I. But I expect I'm going to find out."

They were about to cross the street when Holly realized that something was happening on the opposite corner. A streetcar had come to a halt at the intersection, and a crowd of people were gathered around the front of it. An ambulance came speeding down Third Street, its lights flashing, quickly followed by two police cars.

"Oh God, there's been an accident," said Matthew. "Somebody's been knocked over."

"Come on," said Tyrone, taking Holly's arm. "We can go in by the back door. You don't want to see this."

But as Tyrone led Holly away from the scene of the accident, the crowds parted as if they had been choreographed, and she could suddenly see quite clearly what had happened. The man she had met in the Bellman's Bookstore, the man with the shaving-brush eyebrows that she had imagined for a moment was David, was lying on the streetcar tracks, on his back, with his arms spread. His face was as pale as a suffering medieval martyr, and his lips were wet with blood. More blood was running across the street and creeping along the pavement, heading southwest.

"Oh, shit," said Matthew, and pressed his hand in front of his mouth and started to retch.

"Come on," said Tyrone.

But Holly couldn't take her eyes away from the vision of the man with the shaving-brush eyebrows and the green Burberry coat just like the one David had worn. The streetcar had rolled over him and stopped and its front wheel was resting in the middle of his chest, so that he was almost cut in half. Pale and martyred as he was, he was staring up at the sky with a strangely confident look in his eyes, as if he were hoping that this had never happened and that it was nothing more than a bad dream.

"Holly, come on," Tyrone urged her.

"No," said Holly. "Wait."

The paramedics were already kneeling down on the pavement and opening up their resuscitation packs, although it was obvious to everybody that the man on the tracks could never survive. Holly heard nothing: She only saw them gesticulate, and silently argue, and hurry backward and forward. The man turned his eyes toward her, and it seemed to Holly as if he were asking her why this had happened, and whether he was imagining it, and if she had been anything to do with it.

She looked down. On the pavement lay the books that he had bought from the Bellman Bookstore, on George Stevens and David O. Selznick. The book about George Stevens had fallen open, and the rain was already crinkling its pages. It was marked with blood, too, in a strange jagged pattern, like a claw, and the claw spread right across a black-and-white photograph of James Dean in *Giant*.

Holly turned to Tyrone and opened and closed her mouth but didn't say anything. She couldn't find the words. Tyrone led her away, holding her elbow firmly, propelling her, until they reached his gallery. Matthew followed close behind.

"Are you all right?" he asked her once they were inside. "Do you want a coffee? A brandy? Another glass of wine?"

"I'm fine. It was the shock, that's all. I saw that guy in the bookstore. I talked to him. I thought—I had the impression that he was David."

Outside, the rain was cascading into the street so much that the stormdrains were overflowing, and the roofs of the passing taxis carried a fine mist of spray. Tyrone knelt down and held both of Holly's hands. "Do you know something?" he said. "I'd give a million dollars if only you could hear my voice."

The Heilshorn Home

Holly arrived at the Heilshorn home a few minutes after three P.M. The rain had long since passed over and the sky was streaked with thin gray clouds, like unraveling wool. The Heilshorn home was right at the end of a new housing development called Hawthorne View, a three-bedroom home with a neatly trimmed lawn and unnaturally bloodred chrysanthemums glittering with raindrops. A girl's pink bicycle lay on its side on the path outside, along with a bracelet of bright plastic beads.

She rang the doorbell. At first there was no answer, but when she rang it again, Mrs. Heilshorn appeared behind the frosted-glass door and opened it.

"Yes?" she said blankly. She was a small woman with intensely black hair and bright red lips. She was wearing a wraparound dress in cerise satin with a large gold brooch in the shape of a spray of roses, and large gold earrings. She had a deep, finely wrinkled cleavage and a sharp little up-tilted nose that said *overcorrective surgery*.

"Mrs. Heilshorn?" Holly produced her ID card.

"Holly Summers, Portland Children's Welfare Department. We have an appointment, if you recall."

"We do? What day is it?"

"Thursday."

"Oh my Lord, I forgot all about it. I'm so sorry. I have a memory like a sieve."

"That's all right, I can be pretty forgetful myself sometimes. Do you mind if I come in?"

"Well, you're welcome, but I'm afraid that Sarah-Jane isn't here right now. She's out playing with friends."

"I do need to see her, Mrs. Heilshorn. Can you tell me where she is?"

"I'm afraid I don't have any idea. Her friend's mother has taken them all out for the day, goodness knows where. Maybe the zoo."

"What time do you expect her back?"

Mrs. Heilshorn shrugged and widened her heavily made-up eyes. "Who knows? She may even sleep over."

Holly stepped into the hallway.

"You won't mind taking off your shoes, will you?" said Mrs. Heilshorn, although it wasn't really a question. Holly slipped out of her pumps and followed her into the sitting room.

"We've just had a new carpet fitted," Mrs Heilshorn explained. "And I do like everything to stay *perfect*, don't you?"

The sitting room looked as if nobody was ever allowed to draw breath in it, let alone sit in it. It was almost psychotically neat and tidy, with a sculptured nylon carpet in the palest of honey colors, wallpaper with brown-and-cream curlicues, and a coffee table with a glass top and fluted brass legs, on which was spread an arrangement of shells and pebbles and a china figurine of a mermaid sitting on a rock, as well as a pristine copy of *Woman's Own* with the cover line *Easier Orgasms!*

Above a sandstone fireplace hung a large reproduction of a Gypsy girl with sultry eyes and a blouse that had slipped down from her shoulder to reveal a single bare breast.

Mrs. Heilshorn perched on the arm of one of the large brown brocade armchairs, crossing her legs as if she were posing for a magazine cover. Holly sat on the couch, opened up her briefcase, and took out her notes. "You know why I'm here, don't you?"

"Well, I know that there was some ridiculous nonsense about Sarah-Jane having bruises."

"Sarah-Jane's phys-ed teacher noticed last Monday that she had bruising around her upper thighs and wrists. Her class teacher has also reported that in recent weeks Sarah-Jane has changed from being one of the most outgoing girls in the fifth grade to one of the quietest and least involved. She's been having no problems at school, either with her classwork or with her relationships with other pupils, so her teacher concluded that something must have upset her at home."

"Such as what?"

"That's what I'd like *you* to tell *me*, Mrs. Heilshorn. Has she had any kind of argument with you or your husband? Is there somebody else in the neighborhood she could have had trouble with? Either a neighbor or one of her friends?"

"She's probably starting her period."

"That's not impossible. She's ten and a half, after all.

Has she mentioned anything to you? Asked you about it?"

Mrs. Heilshorn shook her head.

"Have you tried to broach the subject yourself? I mean, given her sudden change in behavior."

"To be honest with you, I can't say that I've noticed *any* change in her behavior. Her teachers might call her 'outgoing,' but as far as my husband and I are concerned, she's never been anything but difficult."

"Really? In what way difficult?"

"Why do you think we've had to go to all the expense of having a new carpet? Sarah-Jane walked in here with her shoes on and tracked in dog mess all over the last one."

She looked around the room with such irritation that Holly half expected to see that the footprints were still there.

"Couldn't you have had it cleaned?"

"*Cleaned?* That would have totally *ruined* it. Have you ever seen what cleaning does to your pile? Flattens it, mats it, makes it go every which way. Maybe a less particular person wouldn't mind about it but *I* always would. I have to have everything—" She didn't actually say the word *perfect* again, but the word was there, hiding behind her pursed red lips.

"I see. What else did Sarah-Jane do that was difficult?"

"Do you want a list? She broke one of my Wedgwood saucers from Woodburn's. Just dropped it on the kitchen floor when she was drying it. She took a peanut butter sandwich to bed and wiped peanut butter all over the throw. That was pure merino wool, that throw.

Do you know what peanut butter does to pure merino wool?"

Holly made some notes while Mrs. Heilshorn arched her neck to try and see what she was writing. "Is that all?" said Mrs. Heilshorn when she had finished.

"I have to ask you about the bruises on Sarah-Jane's thighs and wrists."

"Riding her bike," said Mrs. Heilshorn, with several emphatic nods.

"Riding her bike?"

"She's always riding her bike. I don't know where she goes off to, half the time. She's supposed to be home, doing her homework and helping with the chores. Well! If you can call breaking one of my Wedgwood saucers from Woodburn's helping with the chores . . . But she rides her bike a lot, and when she rides her bike, I guess her thighs get a little bruised. Have you ever seen a kid with no bruises? I never saw a kid with no bruises. When I was her age, I was one big bruise all over. You wouldn't think I was such a tomboy, would you, to look at me now? How old do you think I am?"

Holly hesitated. "I really couldn't say, Mrs. Heilshorn. What about the bruises on her wrists? Did she get those from riding her bike too?"

Mrs. Heilshorn gave an exaggerated shrug. "Maybe some boy tried to grab her."

"Does she have a boyfriend to your knowledge?"

"She *knows* boys—of course she does. I'm forty-one next September twelfth."

"I'll have to talk to her personally, Mrs. Heilshorn. Can we make another appointment?"

"I don't know what Sarah-Jane can possibly tell you that I can't."

"It's routine, Mrs. Heilshorn. If a teacher or a doctor expresses any concern about a child's well-being, we have to investigate. I'm sure you can understand why."

"Listen, I can assure you that nobody's *done* anything to her."

"I didn't suggest that anybody had. But I do have to see her for myself. How about tomorrow, same time?"

"Well, no, that wouldn't be convenient. I have to take her to see my mother in Fairview."

"All right, Monday. But I don't want to postpone it any longer than that."

Mrs. Heilshorn showed her to the door. As Holly was putting her pumps back on, Mrs. Heilshorn said, "Nobody's hurt her, you know. I can promise you that."

Holly didn't reply. But she looked at Mrs. Heilshorn and she saw something in her eyes that seriously disturbed her. She had seen it so many times before, and its name was panic.

Crossing the Burnside Bridge

As she was crossing the Burnside Bridge on her way back to the office, the sun came out and the river glittered as if it were filled with shoals of jumping salmon. Halfway across the bridge, however, she became aware that while everything around her was sparkling in sunshine—the river, the riverside park, the seagoing ships tied up along the waterfront, the Portland Center, and the downtown high-rise towers—she herself was in shadow.

She looked up through the sunroof to see if there was a cloud above her, but the glass was tinted and so it was impossible to tell. But the shadow followed her all the way across the bridge and into the city until she turned left on Broadway. As she slowed down, she could actually see it gliding westward along the facades of the buildings, like the sail of a black yacht.

Suspicious Minds

Doug was tilted back in his chair, reading a thick new report on the psychology of child abusers and eating a sugary doughnut. Through his window Holly could see treetops waving in the wind and silently sliding streetcars and people ambling up and down the sidewalks.

"Hi, Doug," she said, sitting on the edge of his desk.

He lifted his doughnut in greeting. "How did things go with the Heilshorns?"

"They didn't. Sarah-Jane wasn't there. Her mother claimed that she forgot the appointment and that Sarah-Jane was out with friends."

"Sarah-Jane Heilshorn . . . she's the bruise girl from Hawthorne Elementary, isn't she?"

"That's right. Her mother said she probably got them from riding her bike."

"Well, maybe she did." Doug tossed the report onto his paper-strewn desk. "Kids get bruises and nine times out of ten they tripped over or fell out of a tree."

"Sure. But her teachers say that she's been exhibiting some behavioral problems too: acting withdrawn, when she usually used to be extrovert."

"You can't read too much into that, either. When my Annie reached puberty, she turned from Shirley Temple into Courtney Love in one weekend."

"I don't know. Her mother seems kind of *edgy* about her, if you know what I mean. And she's a very obsessive personality. The house is so damn clean, it gave me the creeps. I mean, like, it's *immaculate,* like a show home."

"Met the father yet?"

"Unh-hunh."

"So what's your gut instinct?"

"Something's wrong in that family, but I'm not at all sure what it is. There's a sexual undertone which I don't like at all. Seminude painting over the fireplace . . . trashy women's magazines lying around: You know, the ones that tell you how to strip for your husband."

"Have you made another appointment?"

"Yes, Monday."

"You don't want to action it sooner?"

Holly thought about it and then she shook her head. "No . . . I haven't even had a chance to talk to Sarah-Jane yet. Besides, I don't want to go crashing in there with accusations of abuse unless I have a whole lot more to go on. All right, Mrs. Heilshorn was edgy, but people *do* get edgy when the Children's Welfare people come knocking on their door. And she may be an obsessive Hooverer, but that's not exactly a felony."

"If it *is* a felony, then my ex certainly wasn't guilty of it."

"I think I need to take this carefully, that's all. One step at a time."

Doug sipped his coffee. "Probably wiser. You remember the Katz family?"

"Must have been before my time."

"I almost lost my job over it, believe me. It must have been, what, six or seven years ago. Mr. and Mrs. Katz lived in the Lloyd District. Mrs. Katz had gone to stay with her sister in Bend, but she and her sister had an argument and Mrs. Katz unexpectedly returned home twenty-four hours early. She came into the bedroom at six o'clock in the morning to find her husband in bed, naked, with their four-year-old daughter.

"There was a furious argument and Mrs. Katz called the cops. Mr. Katz was immediately arrested on a charge of suspected molestation, and forensic evidence showed that there were traces of semen on the sheets. My senior director sat in on the police questioning, and she decided that Mr. Katz was protesting his innocence so angrily that he simply had to be guilty."

"Pretty contradictory conclusion."

"Well, she was what you might call an aggressive supporter of women's rights. She believed that all men are rapists, especially husbands and fathers. At first the little girl herself wouldn't say what had happened to her. But after more than a week of very low-key questioning, she blurted out that she had been scared by an electric storm and had crept into her father's bed for security. He had been fast asleep all the time and had never even known she was there.

"The semen?"

"His wife had been away for a week. He had jerked himself off before he went to sleep."

"So what was the outcome?"

"What do you think? Divorce. Mr. Katz couldn't forgive his wife for thinking that he would ever touch his own daughter. So the little girl suffered a broken home just because her mother and the cops and the Children's Welfare Department were all too goddamn eager to believe the worst."

"So . . . your senior director?"

"Not fired, of course, because of the feminist mafia. But moved sideways. These days, she runs Women's Right to Refuse."

"What happened to Women's Right to Say 'Mmm, Yes, Please'?"

Doug brushed sugar off his pants. "You'll keep me posted with the Heilshorn case? I mean, regardless of what happened in the Katz case, any serious suspicions . . ."

"Sure, of course." Holly stood up, and hesitated. "Actually, there's another reason I wanted to see you. What time are you leaving for the lake Saturday?"

"Ten-thirty." Pause. "You mean you want to come along?"

"Yes . . . I think I'd like to."

"That's great. Ned's going to be delighted. He's a really regular guy, I promise you."

"Okay, then. I'll come. Do you want me to bring any food?"

"Hey, only if some of Marcella's spicy meatballs are going begging."

The Doctor Is Out

Holly asked Emma on the switchboard to find the number of East Portland Memorial and to ask for the children's cancer clinic.

"They say wait one moment," said Emma. She was very pretty, intensely black, and had her hair braided in colored beads. Her cotton dress was Barbie-doll pink.

Holly waited and waited. "What's happening?" she asked at last.

"They're playing 'Monday, Monday' by the Mamas and the Papas. You should thank your lucky stars you can't hear nothing."

Holly waited another minute. Just as she was about to give up, Emma said, "Yes, please. I'm calling for Ms. Holly Summers of the Portland Children's Welfare Department. She wants to speak to Dr. Ferdinand. It concerns one of his patients, Casper Beale. B-E-A-L-E. That's right."

Another long wait, then, "Yes, I see. Okay, yes."

Emma looked up at Holly. "Dr. Ferdinand is in San Diego till Monday morning, but his secretary promises to have him call us as soon as he gets back."

"In that case, I'm out of here."

A Puzzle and
Another Shadow

She spent most of Friday morning on paperwork and answering her emails, and she ate a Swiss cheese sandwich at her desk. At three o'clock, as she left the office, she met George Greyeyes in the corridor, impatiently waiting for an elevator.

"Any more news about Daniel Joseph?" he asked her. He looked tired.

"I called the hospital this morning. He's stable but still critical. They're going to operate on his eye tomorrow, if he's well enough."

George checked his watch. "Shit, I'm running late again."

"Another committee meeting?"

"This month's update on anti-Indian prejudice in the Portland Public Schools."

"Uh-huh."

George checked his watch yet again. "These damn elevators. By the way, somebody was asking me about you."

"Oh, yes?"

"An attorney from Mayfield & Letterman, I think it was. He was interested to know who you were."

"Did he say why?"

George shrugged. "I don't think it was anything to do with any particular case. He asked me if you were married, which I thought was kind of strange. And then he asked me where you lived. I didn't tell him, of course."

"What was he like, this attorney?"

"Young, thirtyish. Black hair, smart suit. Quarter Hispanic, maybe. Red and yellow necktie, silk."

"And he didn't give you his name?"

"Not that I recall."

The elevator arrived at last, but they still had to wait while a janitor maneuvered his cleaning cart out of it, all dangling mops and disinfectant sprays and brushes.

"Are you in town for the weekend?" asked George as they descended to the lobby.

"No . . . I'm going to Mirror Lake with Katie and Doug."

"Oh, that's a pity. The National Indian Child Welfare Association is holding a traditional Wallowa cookout Sunday afternoon at Henry High Elk's house. Face decoration, carving displays, rain dancing. I was hoping that you could have come."

"Maybe some other time, George," she said, standing on tiptoe to kiss his cheek. "Sorry."

She left the building and walked out into the breezy street. She still had half an hour before she was due to meet Mickey, so she crossed over to Schnadel's

German-Style Bakery and bought two of the frosted apple strudels that Daisy liked so much.

"You want the extra whipped cream, Ms. Summers?" asked Mr. Schnadel. There were so many mirrors behind his counter that it looked as if there were twenty Mr. Schnadels, all fat-bottomed, with white aprons and white paper hats. "A few hundred calories— what harm did that ever do? Just look at me: I always have the extra whipped cream, and did you ever meet anybody as happy as me?"

Holly smiled. "Happiness? It's that easy? A little extra whipped cream?"

"Sure. The secret about happiness is, don't expect too much from it. It's like luck. People always say, 'I never have good luck.' But they're alive, right? And they have their own teeth. What more good luck do you want than that?"

"What about *bad* luck?"

"*Oh*, no." Mr. Schnadel noisily licked his fingers. "Bad luck is something different."

"What do you mean?"

"Bad luck, it *follows* you. Bad luck is like one of those sniffing dogs, like they use for chasing criminals. Once bad luck picks up your smell, it keeps on coming after you, day after day. *Sniff-sniff-sniff*. Never lets up. Never lets you alone."

"So how can a person shake it off?"

Mr. Schnadel tied a neat bow on top of the cake box and curled the ribbon with his scissor blades. "Shake it off? You can't. You can only hope that one day it's going to grow bored of you and go sniffing after some other unfortunate soul."

Holly stepped out of Schnadel's onto the sidewalk, into the wind. Before she crossed the street, she turned back to see Mr. Schnadel talking to another customer. She felt oddly disturbed by what he had said to her. What did a man who baked cream cakes for a living know about bad luck, and how it came panting after you, and never gave you peace?

She was halfway across the road when her eye was caught by a quick, flickering movement in front of the office building. At first it looked like somebody running across the entrance to the parking levels in the basement. A panel van sped in front of her, blocking her view for an instant. By the time the van had passed, the figure was already running down the parking ramp. It was *dancing*, maybe, rather than running, and it was more like a shadow than a real person: black, and distorted, and very tall, with ragged arms and legs. She saw it dance against the concrete wall at the back of the ramp, and then it was gone.

She took a step forward and it was then that a bicycle hit her and she was thrown sideways into the road, jarring her shoulder against the asphalt. Her ribbon-tied box of apple strudel flew across the road and a car drove over it and emphatically squashed it. At first she didn't understand what had happened to her. She saw sky . . . asphalt . . . and somebody leaning over her, a man with a gingery mustache. He was saying something to her but she couldn't tell what it was.

The man with the gingery mustache took her by the elbow and helped her onto her feet. He smelled of cigarettes and cheap aftershave. She wasn't badly hurt, but all the breath had been knocked out of her. The bike rider was sitting only a few feet away, a young hawk-nosed man in a shocking-pink space-age cycling helmet and tight black cycling shorts. He was frantically spinning his front wheel, around and around, and saying, "Oh God. Oh God. Don't tell me the spokes are out of alignment."

Holly turned around to the man with the gingery mustache and said, "Thanks. Thank you." He lifted his cap with old-fashioned courtesy and said something in reply, but again she couldn't quite catch it. She went over to the bike rider and smacked him on the shoulder. He looked up at her irritably and said, "What?"

"You hit me," she said. "You ran me down, you maniac."

"Hey, I rang my fucking bell, didn't I? I shouted, 'Look out!'—didn't I? What are you, deaf?"

The Other Side of Luck

When she walked into the Compass Hotel, Mickey was almost too sympathetic.

"Hey, what the hell happened to you?" he said, putting his arm around her.

She winced and pointed to her shoulder. "I had an argument with a cyclist and the cyclist won."

Mickey stopped and turned back toward the street, his neck as taut as a Doberman's. "Where? Where is he? I'll break his fucking legs."

"He's *gone*, Mickey, and in any case it was my fault for crossing the road without looking."

"What did he look like? Give me a description and I'll have him pulled in."

"Forget it, will you? I'm okay. All I need to do is tidy myself up."

Holly went to the hotel restroom. She took off her coat and pulled up her pale green sweater to check her shoulder. Her skin was reddened and slightly grazed, even though her coat and her sweater hadn't been torn. She dabbed it with a wet towel. It looked as if she was going to have an attractive multicolored bruise on her back when she went up to Mirror Lake that weekend, a map of Alaska in varying shades of purple.

She leaned on the basin and stared at herself in the mirror. She didn't *look* shaken, even though she was— and badly. It wasn't just being knocked over that had upset her: It was the feeling that the world around her had suddenly been altered, and that she had lost her sense of certainty. It was at times like these that her deafness frustrated her to the point of screaming, even though she wouldn't have been able to hear herself. She felt as if she were sitting alone in the next room while the rest of the human race giggled and whispered and conspired together. Why did everybody rush out and buy a pop song one particular week? Holly would never know, because she couldn't hear it, and she didn't know why it had caught everybody's mood. Not only that, she would never have a favorite love song.

You're feeling sorry for yourself, she told her reflection in the mirror.

No, I'm not, her reflection replied. *I'm afraid, but I don't exactly know why.*

She brushed her hair, fixed her lipstick, and then rejoined Mickey in the glossy black-marble foyer. He was talking on his cell phone. "They found a shoe? Where? Well, I'm coming back to headquarters later; I'll take a look at it."

He snapped his phone shut and said, "Sarah Hargitay. They think they found one of her shoes up near Bridal Veil."

"All the way up the valley? What was she doing there?"

"Hobbling, I expect."

They walked through to the Sternwheeler Bar. Mickey guided her off to the left, into a semicircular booth upholstered in chestnut-brown leather with a brass-bound mahogany table. The bar was decorated to resemble the saloon of an old-style riverboat, with gilded pillars and railings and paintings of voluptuous nudes stretched out on divans, and there were huge mirrors on every wall. A pianist in a green eyeshade was playing Scott Joplin melodies as if he were more used to chopping up spare ribs. Through the panoramic windows on the right-hand side of the bar, Holly could see the whole of the Portland waterfront, with white yachts dipping and bobbing at anchor and a large oceangoing timber ship slowly gliding past, its flanks streaked with rust.

"Krauss is sitting behind that plant on the far side of the piano. He knows what he's doing. The CCTV can't cover him from there, and the piano's too loud for us to pick him up clearly with a directional mike."

Holly stood up and looked airily around the bar as if she were expecting somebody. She could just see Merlin Krauss sitting at a table by the window, wearing a loud yellow coat. On one side he was flanked by a hard-faced young Chinese in an expensive light-gray suit, on the other by a huge man in a tight black T-shirt, with a flattop and a broken nose.

"All human life is there," Mickey remarked as Holly sat down again. "The Chink on the left is Danny Hee, who's into anything from crack cocaine to fake Rolexes.

The big ape on the right is Vernon Pulitzer, who used to be a boxer but is actually gay. You going to be okay with this? You want a drink?"

"Just a coffee, thanks."

Mickey said, "You see that table for two, right opposite Krauss? You can sit there and pretend that you've been stood up, or that you're a lonely spinster or something. You can sit facing the mirror, with your back to him, so it won't be so obvious that you're watching him. You'll also be well out of earshot, so hopefully he won't be inhibited about talking business. Maybe, with any luck, he'll talk about this hit he's arranging too."

"Do you believe in luck?"

"Luck? For sure. I wouldn't spend so much of my salary at Portland Meadows if I didn't."

"What about *bad* luck? Do you believe in that?"

He caught something in the tone of her voice and narrowed his eyes. "Is something worrying you?"

"I don't know. I never believed in bad luck before. I couldn't, could I, after losing my hearing? The only way to deal with it was to count my blessings and try to think that God had made me deaf for a very good reason."

"But now?"

"Now I'm not so sure. I feel like everything's changed but I don't quite know how. It's like walking into a room and somebody's moved all the furniture and the pictures but you can't remember how they were before, except that you find it disturbing."

"You're giving me the creeps, you know that?"

The waitress came over to take their order. After she had gone, Mickey leaned forward and said, "I used to know a detective called Frank Fraser who always carried this two-headed quarter as a lucky charm. We were going into a warehouse on the waterfront once, me and Frank. Somebody had tipped us off that it was full of contraband booze and cigarettes. We climbed up onto the building next door so that we could jump across onto the roof.

"I went first, but I landed badly and my shoe came off. Frank came after me, and he was laughing at me while I was hopping around on one leg, trying to get my shoe back on. He opened the door that led down into the warehouse and *bang!* I'll never forget it as long as I live. His head blew up like a bunch of red roses.

"So what was that? Bad luck for Frank but good luck for me." He reached into his pocket and took out a coin. "This is it: This is Frank's two-headed quarter. I carried it ever since, to remind me that every situation has two sides to it, and that one day it might be me who opens the door first. Bad luck, good luck. Who knows which is which?"

Merlin Talks Business

Holly went over to the table opposite Merlin Krauss and the waitress brought her a tiny cup of espresso and a small plateful of almond madeleines. Merlin was drinking Full Sail ale and eating handfuls of nuts as if he needed them to stay alive. Danny Hee was complaining about something, while Vernon Pulitzer was staring into the middle distance and solemnly concentrating on picking his left nostril.

She couldn't pick up everything that Merlin was saying, particularly since he kept clapping his hand in front of his mouth to fill it with nuts, and lipreading in a mirror was always slightly more problematic than lipreading full-face. Nobody's mouth was perfectly symmetrical, as Holly used to demonstrate by challenging people to curl their lips like Elvis on *both* sides of their face.

"No—I never guaranteed no specific date," Merlin insisted, chewing nuts and shaking his head from side to side. "I guaranteed a delivery, yes, but I never guaranteed no specific date."

"What good is it saying you're going to deliver when you can't say *when* you're going to deliver?"

"I'm *going* to deliver. I *guaranteed* to deliver. But I never guaranteed no specific date."

"So when? Tomorrow?"

"I don't know, Danny. Do I look like some kind of fucking clairvoyant? I mean, do you see any crystal balls around here?"

"Where's the stuff now?"

"It's *coming*, Danny. Trust me. It's on its way."

"So when?"

"I told you. You'll get your delivery. You've paid for it, you'll get it. Did I ever let you down before?"

"No, but when? Next week? I have to have it by the end of next week or else I'm fucked."

"Listen—I'm not going to let you pin me down to some specific date because I never guaranteed no specific date. Who do you have on your back anyhow, it's all got to be so fucking urgent? Not that Sung asshole?"

Danny Hee said nothing.

"It's Sung, isn't it, that asshole? What an asshole. Thinks he's in a Jackie Chan movie. Well, you can tell him from me that he'll get what's coming when it comes. Asshole."

Holly was used to the repetitive monotony of criminals' conversation. It was tedious, but it made it easier to fill in the words that she inevitably missed. It was never like a Quentin Tarantino movie, no witty observations about what Big Macs were called in Paris. It was all "a deal's a deal, right? Understand what I mean? Like, when I say it's a deal, it's a deal." And "my son's playing basketball tonight, he's doing great, he's really doing great."

"Yeah?" "Yeah, he's really doing great." "Yeah? Great."

Even when they were discussing acts of extreme violence or bizarre sexual practices, criminals were invariably boring and matter-of-fact. She had once lip-read the conversation between two men who were going to take their revenge on a friend for sleeping with one of their wives. They had talked about cutting off his penis and stuffing it in his mouth as if they were discussing a trip to Freddy's supermarket.

"So we'll cut it off, okay, and you can open his mouth and I can push it down his throat."

"You could choke him, doing that."

She sat there for nearly an hour and a half, drinking two more cups of coffee and irritably checking her watch as if she were waiting for a friend to show up. Two or three times Mickey appeared in the background and raised his eyebrows to ask her if Merlin had said anything in relation to the hit. Each time she had to shake her head.

Danny Hee eventually left, still complaining about his delivery. Merlin sat eating nuts and saying nothing for almost ten minutes, while Vernon Pulitzer transferred his attention to excavating his ears. It was well past six o'clock now and Holly had to be home by seven to give Daisy something to eat and to pack her weekend case. She was just about to leave when Merlin picked up his cell phone.

"Yeah? What? Oh, it's you, Mr Rossabi. Yeah, fine. You don't have to worry. Everything's under control. Four o'clock Tuesday afternoon, just like you said, right outside the Richard Herrera Hair Salon, Southwest Main. Richard Herr-*era*."

He paused, listening, and then he said, "What did I tell you? Not a trace."

Another pause, then, "Like I said before, it's better that you don't know. I wouldn't tell you over the phone even if I would tell you, which I won't. Okay? I'm sorry, you're going to have to be happy with that. Yeah. No. That's right. You won't know she even existed."

A very much longer pause, and then, "Let me put it this way, Mr. Rossabi. I have a friend in the wood-pulping business. She's going to make the front page of *The Oregonian*. Literally."

Holly waited for three or four more minutes, and then she got up to leave. As she passed Merlin's table, he said, "Never showed, then, the sap?"

"What?"

"Your date, he never showed. What a sap. Lovely-looking woman like yourself, if you don't mind my saying so."

"Thank you. I guess his plane was delayed."

Merlin offered his cell phone. "Want to call him? Be my guest."

"That's all right, thank you."

"What's your name, if you don't mind my asking."

"Margaret."

"Well, nice to meet you, Margaret. I hope you don't think I'm sneaky or nothing, but I've been checking you in the mirror ever since you sat down, and I have an inkling that you were checking *me* out, once or twice, weren't you? You're a lovely-looking woman. Unforgettable. I hope to see you again."

"Why not?" said Holly.

Fallen Moon

Mickey was waiting for her on the steps outside the hotel, smoking. "So, how did it go?" he asked her, laying his hand on her shoulder.

"*Ouch*," she protested.

"Sorry—forgot about the bruise. Did you pick up anything good?"

"Well, it took some time, but I think so. Krauss came out with a name, somebody called Rossabi. He also mentioned a time and a date, and Richard Herrera's Hair Salon on Southwest Main. I even think I know what they're planning to do with the body."

"You're amazing. You know that? You're absolutely amazing. Listen—why don't we go to the Rock Bottom Brewery and we can have a serious debriefing over a serious beer?"

"I can't. I have to go home and give Daisy her supper."

She had just climbed into Mickey's car, however, when her cell phone warbled, and it was a text message from Daisy. "Mom. Tracey hs asked me 2 play & she hs

SpongeBob Barbie so can I?" This was immediately followed by "Its OK by me, XX Evelyn. Home by 8."

She showed the messages to Mickey. "What would *you* say?"

"I'd say that we have time for that beer."

But they were just turning onto Southwest Morrison when Mickey picked up his radio and started talking into it. Holly could see him say, "Harris can't handle it? I'm real tied up here."

He paused and frowned, and then he said, "Names?"

Another pause. "Never heard of either of them."

He nodded and said, "Okay. Okay, I'll get right over there."

"Problem?" asked Holly.

"Yes . . . I'm sorry. I'm going to have to drop you off. There's been a shooting at the Deh-Ta Grocery Store in Chinatown. One individual killed, another one seriously wounded. Somebody at headquarters seems to think that they're friends of mine." He frowned again, thinking, but then he shook his head. "Some guy called Gerald Butler and some other guy called Kevin McKenna. Never heard of either of them."

"Do you want me to come along?"

"You can if you like. It shouldn't take me very long."

"Then I'll come along."

When they reached Chinatown they found the whole block sealed off and seven squad cars parked across the street with their lights flashing, as well as two ambulances and a TV truck. Mickey led Holly through the police barrier and up to the front of the Deh-Ta Grocery Store. The grocery's front was painted in red and gold, and most of the window was crowded with Chinese posters and postcards and dangling dolls and decorations.

Inside, there was a glass counter on the right and a long central aisle crammed with bottles of rice wine and cans of smoked oysters and boxes of Chinese spices. Three floodlights had been positioned around the store so that it looked dazzlingly bright, like a movie set: INT. CHINESE GROCERY STORE. NIGHT.

Seven or eight police officers and paramedics were standing in the aisle in front of the counter, talking in the casual way that people who are used to human tragedy always do. On the wooden floor in front of them lay the body of an overweight young man in his late twenties, wearing faded blue jeans and a white shirt with splashy red poppies on it, except that they weren't splashy red poppies: They were blood. Holly could see his pale hairy belly bulging over his belt.

A stocky, gray-haired man in a crumpled gray linen coat came out of the store. "Mickey . . . hi. Thanks for dropping by." He looked Holly up and down. "Didn't want to screw up your evening or anything."

"This is Holly Summers. She's our consultant lipreader."

"Oh, *right*. I heard about her. The deaf lady. You used her on the Steelhead Cannery case, didn't you? Classic bust, that. Classic. I don't know how she did it."

"Jack, she may be deaf, but she can understand what you're saying, and believe it or not she can speak."

"Oh, sorry. Tell her I'm sorry."

Mickey pointed to Holly, and Jack Harris gave her

a quick, embarrassed glance and muttered, "Sorry."

"So what's happening here? Who are these guys that are supposed to be friends of mine?"

"It was a robbery that went wrong. Three guys came into the store, one of them stood by the door to stop anybody else from coming in, the other two went up to Mr. Deh-Ta and told him to open the register."

"Were they armed?"

"Mr. Deh-Ta said that one of them was holding something black that looked like an automatic weapon. He said he was frightened for his life, so he took out his pump-action shotgun from under the counter and let the guy have it, point-blank range in the chest. The second guy ran for the door but Mr. Deh-Ta shot him in the back. Lucky for the second guy that Mr. Deh-Ta is a lousy shot: It only took half his shoulder off."

"That sounds like pretty good luck to me," said Mickey, looking at Holly. "Did you recover the automatic weapon?"

Jack Harris lifted his left hand. Dangling from his index finger was a black collapsible umbrella.

"You could do a lot of serious damage with that," Mickey remarked.

"Depends where you put it before you opened it up."

Mickey looked around. "So who said these guys were friends of mine? What did you say their names were?"

"Gerald Butler is the dead guy. Kevin McKenna is the guy with no shoulder. It was McKenna who said you were friends of theirs." Pause. "Well, obviously."

Mickey said to Holly, "Wait here a second, will you?"

He went into the store and edged his way through the cops and the paramedics. Holly could see him hunkering down beside the body. After a while he stood up and edged his way out again.

"August Moon," he said, with a peculiar cough.

"What?"

"Gerald Butler is part of a Chinese transvestite act who call themselves the Three Concubines. His stage name is August Moon. Kevin McKenna is Lotus Flower, and the third guy was probably Bruce."

Jack Harris took out his notebook. "You know something? The longer I live, the more I see, the less I don't fucking believe it."

"They wouldn't have hurt a fly. They'd had some bad luck getting bookings, that's all. This, ah . . . Mr. Deh-Ta—he still around?"

"Sure. He's in the squad car over there."

"Mind if I talk to him for a minute?"

"Be my guest."

Mickey held up his wristwatch and tapped the crystal to indicate to Holly that he wouldn't be long. He went over to the squad car and climbed into the rear seat next to Mr. Deh-Ta. Holly couldn't see much of Mr. Deh-Ta because of the reflected light against the curving window, but he looked thin and fiftyish, with wiry hair sticking up.

Jack Harris suddenly turned to Holly and shouted, *"You really that deaf? Like, ah, I don't want to be personal or nothing!"* She could tell by the excited look on his face that he was quite pleased with himself for talking to her, as if he had plucked up the courage to have a conversation with somebody in a wheelchair.

"Totally deaf," she smiled. "So there's no need for you to shout."

"Oh," he blinked. Then, cunningly, "How did you know I was shouting?"

"Because your face went bright red and everybody else turned around to look at you."

"Oh."

She turned to see what Mickey was doing. Although the inside of the squad car was so dark, a curve of light illuminated Mickey's lips, and now and then Mr. Deh-Ta turned halfway toward her too. She couldn't pick up everything that Mickey was saying, but the expression on his face said it all.

"So how much did you have in the register?"

Head shake.

"How much did you have in the register, Mr. Deh-Ta? I want to know how much you had in the register."

"Hundred dollar. Maybe hundred twenty-five and change."

"You killed a guy for a hundred twenty-five and change? You fucking *killed* him?"

"—gun—"

"What, are you blind? That wasn't a gun, that was a fucking *umbrella*. Do you ever watch TV?"

Head shake.

"I said, do you ever watch TV? Do you watch cop shows? Ever seen a cop show? *NYPD Blue,* anything like that?"

"He ask for money. He say give me all your money."

"With an *umbrella*, Mr. Deh-Ta! You ever seen the bad guys in *NYPD Blue* pulling umbrellas? 'Give me all your money, or else I'll make sure that you don't get wet!'?"

Holly started to smile, but then she saw Mickey take hold of Mr. Deh-Ta's necktie and shake the Chinaman's head from side to side. She looked around for Jack Harris, but he had gone back inside the store.

Mickey's face was as hard as riven slate. "You killed a guy, Mr. Deh-Ta, and you took half another guy's arm off, because you didn't fucking look and you didn't fucking *think*. And do you know what's going to happen to you? Nothing, that's what's going to happen to you. In fact, they'll probably give you a fucking medal."

Mickey stopped for breath, and then he slammed Mr. Deh-Ta's head back against the headrest. Holly saw Mickey's mouth shouting, "He was a human being! He was a human being! You just don't get it, do you! He was somebody's son!"

She walked quickly over to the squad car and rapped on the window. Mickey immediately let go of Mr. Deh-Ta's necktie and made of show of tugging his shirt collar straight. At that moment Jack Harris came back out of the store, writing in his notebook.

Mickey climbed out of the far side of the car. He smoothed back his hair with both hands and buttoned up his coat. Holly stared at him and she didn't know what to say. He simply raised one eyebrow, as if to say "What?"

Jack Harris opened up the nearside door and helped Mr. Deh-Ta to climb out. Mr. Deh-Ta looked confused and bewildered, and when Mickey came around the car toward him he lifted one elbow as if to protect himself.

"Don't worry about a thing, Mr. Deh-Ta," said Mickey, slapping him on the back. "You're a hero."

• • •

On the way home, Mickey turned to Holly and said, "You're quiet."

"I don't know. I guess I'm a little shocked, that's all."

"Because I gave that guy a hard time?"

"Because I'm seeing a side of you I never saw before. First Elliot Joseph, now this guy."

Mickey thought about that for a while, and then he said, "I'm a cop, Holly. That means I get paid to uphold the law. But there's law and there's justice, and believe me, they're two different ball games.

"August Moon . . . he was one of the gentlest people on the planet. You want to talk about law? Okay, August Moon broke the law. But you want to talk about justice? He was executed without a trial. He was executed for being different, and for finding it difficult to make a living. All over America, every day of the week, people *murder* people and they don't get executed. But August Moon tried to steal a hundred twenty-five bucks with a collapsible umbrella and that was it. The death sentence."

He drew up outside Torrefazione. "I'm sorry. You shouldn't have seen what happened tonight. You did very good work at the Compass. . . . You've probably saved a woman's life."

"I have to go in now. Daisy will be home soon."

All the same, she stayed where she was and looked at him for almost half a minute without saying anything, and he looked back at her.

"I hope, ah . . . ," Mickey began, and then stopped.

"You hope what?"

"I hope what happened with Elliot Joseph, and back there at Deh-Ta's . . . I hope you're not starting to think that I'm some kind of psycho."

She smiled and shook her head. "I can understand why you lost your temper. I think I might have done the same."

"You? I can't imagine you angry."

"Oh, you wouldn't like me when I'm angry."

"What would you do?" asked Mickey. "Turn green and throw a bus at me?"

"No. I'd stop reading your lips, that's all."

"Whoo. That would shut me up, wouldn't it?"

"As far as *I'm* concerned, totally."

Mickey reached out and gently fingered her hair. "This isn't an easy thing to say. I mean, however I put it, it's going to sound patronizing."

"Go on," she encouraged him.

"The whole thing is . . . I like you, Holly. I really like you for who you are. It's no good me trying to pretend that it doesn't matter, you being deaf. Like, it's part of the reason I like you so much: the fact that you're deaf and yet, the way that you deal with it."

He clenched his fist and knocked himself twice on the forehead. "Shit, that came out wrong."

Holly smiled. "I like you, too, Mickey."

"But what?"

"I didn't say *but*. It's just that I don't know you very well. After this evening, less than I thought."

"But you still like me?"

She hesitated, and then she kissed him on the cheek.

Daisy Sulks

Friday was Marcella's evening off, so Holly went down to Torrefazione downstairs and brought up pepperoni pizza with extra black olives. It was fresh and hot, but Daisy ate only one slice of hers and then prodded at the rest with her fork, swinging one leg under the table.

Holly watched her for a while and then said, "You don't like it? I could get you something else instead. Maybe some linguine?"

Daisy shrugged and continued prodding and swinging.

"Now you're not talking to me? What? You're annoyed that I'm going away for the weekend?"

Another shrug. Holly finished her mouthful and said, "Listen, I haven't had a break for over a year. I deserve a break, quite frankly. And you don't mind spending the weekend with Gillian, do you? If you do, why didn't you say so before I made the arrangement?"

"I don't mind spending the weekend with Gillian, okay?"

"So what's wrong? Tell me, I'm your mother."

"It's nothing."

"It's *nothing?* So why are you behaving like a ballet dancer with a sore butt?"

Daisy glowered at her from under her eyebrows but didn't answer.

"You all finished, then?" Holly asked her. "You're excused from the table. You can wash your plate and put it away and then you can go pack for tomorrow. And don't take that yellow skirt with the frills: It's too small for you and it makes you look like a human daffodil."

Daisy sulked off into the kitchen. Holly sat at the dining table alone, trying to finish her pizza, but she didn't have the appetite for it anymore. She pushed her plate away and poured herself another glass of wine. Under her breath she sang, *"What is your one-o? Green grow the rushes-o. One is one and all alone and ever more shall be so."* She could hear it in her head but she couldn't hear her own voice.

Tears at Bedtime

Holly packed the smart green weekend bag that Tyrone had bought her at the Columbia Sportswear Company, and then she went to see how Daisy was managing. Daisy was sitting on the end of her bed with a heap of clothes strewn all over it, and only a Princess Barbie and two pairs of panties in her case.

"Come on, I'll help you," said Holly.

"I can do it."

"Okay, but if you're going to do it, do it. I want you to get an early night tonight."

She waited, but Daisy made no effort to finish her packing. In the end she sat down beside her and said, "What's wrong? Come on, pumpkin, you can tell me what it is, whatever it is."

Daisy looked at her and her eyes were filling up with tears. "I miss my daddy," she said.

Holly put her arm around her and hugged her. Daisy was so outspoken and sure of herself that sometimes she forgot how young she was, how vulnerable. "I know you do, pumpkin. I miss him too."

"Do you have to go to Mirror Lake with Katie and Doug? Couldn't you go someplace else?"

"You don't want me to go to Mirror Lake? Is that what this is all about?"

"I don't want you to go with Ned."

"But why? You don't even know Ned. Neither do I."

"I just don't like the sound of him. Ned. He sounds like a horse."

"He's probably okay. Katie thinks I'm really going to like him."

"That's the trouble."

Holly reached over to Daisy's nightstand and plucked out a Kleenex. She dabbed at Daisy's eyes and then said, "Blow. That's better. Now are you going to tell me why you don't want me to go with Ned?"

"Because of Uncle Mickey. If you like Ned, then you won't go out with Uncle Mickey anymore."

"I see. You really like Uncle Mickey, huh?"

Daisy flushed and nodded.

"I like Uncle Mickey too. But we're not dating or anything like that. We work together, that's all, and I like to think that we're friends, but that's about as far as it goes."

"You don't have to marry him or anything."

"Oh, thanks."

Daisy was almost hurting with the effort to explain what she meant. "It's just that he reminds me of dad. I mean, he doesn't *look* like dad, but when he's here—when he came to supper and told me that story—he *felt* like dad."

To her surprise, Holly suddenly found that she had tears in her eyes too. She stroked Daisy's forehead and said, "Yes. Yes, I know what you're saying."

A Night Visitor

There was no moon that night and the apartment was intensely dark. Holly lay awake until nearly two-thirty in the morning, watching the red numbers on her bedside alarm clock counting away her life. She had promised Daisy that she would do everything humanly possible not to like Ned, and that even if she did, she would still invite Uncle Mickey round for supper and let him stay to tell her bedtime stories.

She heard a ship hooting mournfully on the river, and then another, as if they were whales mating.

She remembered waking up one morning to find David sitting in the white-painted rocker by the bedroom window, his eyes narrowed, looking through the two-inch gap between the blind and the windowsill. He seemed to be waiting.

"David?" she had asked him. At that instant he had whipped his head sideways, his eyes tightly shut, as if something were flying directly toward his face.

Six days later he was dead. She often wondered if he

had experienced a premonition of what was going to happen to him.

The bedside clock flicked to 2:33. Holly turned onto her back and stared up into the darkness. This is what it must be like, being blind.

As she lay there, however, she became aware that there was an even darker darkness, and it appeared to be hovering right over her. It kept shifting its shape, but it looked as if it had outspread wings and was steadying itself in some unfelt updraft.

The longer she stared at it, the blacker it became, black and ruffled like a monstrous bird. She knew that there was nothing there. How could a giant raven be flying over her bed? Yet, she was sure that she could see it rising and falling and constantly altering its appearance, and she began to feel a chilly dread of what it was going to do to her.

She carefully reached out with one hand toward the nightstand. She found the cable that led to her bedside lamp and tried to locate the switch. Up above her the dark shape spread wider until it was covering almost the entire ceiling.

She found the switch, and she was just about to turn on the light when the shape *dropped* on her with a rush of feathers and freezing-cold wind. She cried out "*Aaahh!*" and threw up her hands to protect her face, knocking the lamp onto the floor.

She waited. Silence. She opened her eyes and gradually lowered her hands. The bedside clock said 2:57. The room was still dark, but she could sense that there was nothing there. She climbed out of bed and groped her way over to the main light switch. When she turned it on, she saw that her sheets were violently twisted, as if she had been fighting, and that the red pottery lamp was broken into three large pieces. David had brought her that lamp from San Francisco.

She went to the bathroom for a drink of water and stared at herself in the mirror. She hadn't noticed before, but she was beginning to get dark circles under her eyes, as if she were ill or very tired.

She was still standing there when Daisy appeared.

"Mommy? I heard something."

She tried to smile. "That was only me. I was having a bad dream just like you did."

"It wasn't you."

Holly turned around and put her hands on Daisy's shoulders. "There's nobody else here, pumpkin. I promise you."

"It wasn't *inside*. It was *outside*, tapping at my window."

"Honey, we're three stories up. Nothing can tap against your window."

"It sounded like a bird."

"A bird? How do you know?"

"I could hear its wings. It was tapping against the window with its beak and it was flapping its wings too."

Holly said nothing but bent forward and kissed the top of Daisy's head.

"It was a bird," Daisy insisted. "It was a bird and it was trying to get in."

Mirror Lake

They reached the cabin at Mirror Lake just before noon. The water was so still that it reflected a perfect upside-down world with dark sawtooth pines and scatterings of red-and-yellow maple leaves. The cabin itself was painted a rusty red, with a gray shingle roof and a veranda running the length of it. It stood on a small promontory on the southeastern side of the lake, next to a sagging wooden jetty where an old green rowboat was tied up.

Doug climbed out of the Voyager and stretched. He was wearing a logger's jacket in orange and brown check, with a lamb's-wool collar and a cap to match. "Smell that ozone! *Haaahh!* Smell that pine! *Haaahh!*"

Katie wore a bulky maroon sweater with elks on it and a knitted hat pulled down low over her forehead, so that she looked like an affluent bag lady. "I thought Ned would be here by now. He only had to drive up from Government Camp. I hope he's *coming.*"

Holly walked to the very edge of the lake. She was wearing black: a black windcheater with a fur hood, black jeans, and black leather boots. Although her world was always silent, she could almost *feel* the silence here. Beyond the lake, above the treeline, Mount Hood loomed, only three and a half miles away, ghostly and grand.

This close, the mountain's gravity was overwhelming, even though its whiteness made it almost invisible. She felt as if it were pulling her toward her destiny with a greater force than ever before.

"What do you think?" asked Doug, joining her at the lakeside.

"It's beautiful. So peaceful."

"You should be here when the geese are mating. It's like a traffic snarl."

Katie called, "Are you going to give me a hand with the shopping, Doug?"

"Sure thing. Did you remember the pickles?"

"I sure did. I bought some of those Rocotillo peppers you like too."

Doug was silent for a moment, and then he said, "My grandfather built this place. He used to say that you could stand by this lake and talk to God."

They carried their bags into the cabin. It was chilly inside, and musty, but as soon as he had taken his case to his bedroom, Doug took the fire screen away from the gray stone hearth and started to build a fire. Katie led Holly through to a small bedroom at the back, with pine furniture, a hand-sewn quilt on the bed, and a view of an overgrown yard, with bracken and rusty-colored ragwort.

On the wall hung a small oil painting of a woman standing in a field. She was wearing a blue apron and a bemused smile, as if she couldn't understand why anybody would think that she was interesting enough to paint. Not far away from her, perched on a single fence post, was a large black bird with ruffled feathers.

Holly went through to the kitchen, where Katie was unpacking the shopping. "We'll go down to Lyman's Hotel for lunch; you'll love it. But this evening I'm going to cook my famous *chuletas veracruzana.*"

In the living room, Doug had already got a good fire crackling. The living room had a high ceiling with exposed rafters and was furnished with big, comfortable couches upholstered in flowery chintz. The rafters were hung with copper pots and pans, and all around the walls there were glass cases containing stuffed fish: salmon, trout, steelhead, and sturgeon.

"My grandfather was mad for fishing," said Doug. "See that baby at the far end? That sturgeon? That weighed nearly fifty pounds."

Suddenly he lifted his finger. "That'll be Ned."

He opened the front door and Holly saw a bronze Land Cruiser parked next to Doug's Voyager. Katie came out of the kitchen and said, "You're going to like this guy, I promise you."

"What did I say?" Holly retorted. "No matchmaking, if you don't mind."

"How about a beer? Come on, I know it's a little early, but this is our weekend off."

"Sure, I'll have a beer."

Doug came back into the cabin, closely followed by Ned. *Well,* thought Holly, *at least he isn't a short, pudgy guy with a comb-over.* In fact he was tall and broad-shouldered, with wavy reddish-blond hair and clear caramel-colored eyes and a square, suntanned face that put Holly in mind of Robert Redford but thirty years younger and with a much thicker neck. He was wearing a navy sports coat, a blue-checkered shirt, and Armani jeans.

"Holly, this is Ned Fiedler. Ned, I'd like you to meet Holly."

Ned nodded and grinned. Then he made both of his hands into Y shapes and made a pulling-apart gesture, after which he pointed directly at Holly and made a circular gesture over his head.

Holly smiled. "I'm sorry . . . I lip-read but I don't sign. Signing has a totally different grammar, and I never needed to learn it."

Ned flushed. He looked helplessly at Doug and said, "What do I do now?"

"You *talk,* that's all," said Holly. "So long as I can see your lips, I can tell what you're saying. And thanks for trying to learn some ASL. . . . That was very considerate of you."

"Was I any good at it?"

"Well, I think you just about managed to say 'How you, big hat?'"

Katie came out of the kitchen with four bottles of Portland Ale. "We're real glad you could make it, Ned. I've been trying to persuade Holly to have a weekend off since Labor Day."

Ned raised his bottle to Holly and said, "I'm glad I could make it too. Here's to us, and here's to having a great time."

"To us," they chorused. "And to having a great time."

Ned Gets Serious

They went for lunch to Lyman's, a pictur-
esque redbrick hotel built in 1905 and surrounded by
larches. It stood on a promontory overlooking the Columbia River Gorge, and through the windows of the
old-fashioned saloon bar they could see the river shining as it ran between the hazy, sun-gilded mountains.
The water was wide here, and it was crisscrossed with
the multicolored sails of sailboards, reds and yellows
and blues.

"You ever tried windsurfing?" Ned asked Holly.
"Amazing sport. Really amazing. And this is the best
place in the whole darn world to do it. You got your
strong, steady winds, anything between fifteen to
thirty-five miles an hour, and at the same time you've
got your strong opposing currents."

"I'm more into cycling. Well, I have a little girl and
most weekends we take our bikes around Forest Park."

"A little girl, huh? How old?"

"She was eight in May. She's very good company."

"You ought to bring her along with you one weekend. I could teach her how to windsurf. You, too, if you like."

"That sounds exciting."

"Oh, believe me."

There was a long silence while Holly picked at her grilled chicken salad with smoky mayonnaise, and Doug made a spectacular mess of his Dungeness crab baguette, dropping lumps of crabmeat onto the table-cloth.

"Doug was raised by warthogs," said Katie. "That's why he eats like that."

"Hey, I enjoy my food," Doug protested. "I *relish* it, unlike you. I like to get physically involved with it."

"So does the front of your sweater."

They drank another toast. Doug put his hand in front of his mouth to suppress a burp, and then there was another long silence. Eventually, Holly said, "So, Ned . . . wood pulp."

He gave her what he obviously believed was a winning smile. "That's right. Wood pulp. Fascinating business, wood pulp."

"What is it you actually do?"

"I'm senior exec in charge of recycling. That means making the best use of residual fiber and other waste materials."

"Oh, right."

He put down his fork, with a neatly cut square of steak still on the end of it. "You see, not many people realize this, but there are all kinds of different waste materials. There's *pre*consumer waste, which is leftover scrap generated in the paper- and box-manufacturing process. That's what we call 'clean' waste. Then there's *post*consumer waste, which is articles that have been used for their intended purpose and are ready to be discarded, such as OCC."

Holly looked blank.

"Sorry—that's short for *old corrugated containers.*"

"I see."

Ned leaned closer. There was a shred of steak caught between his two front teeth. "Recycling is far more important than biodegradability, because very few items are actually biodegradable with current landfill practices. What I aim to do, Holly, is to capture used items *before* they reach the landfill and put them to their best possible use."

"You make it sound like a mission."

"It *is* a mission, Holly. You're right. At Hood River Forestry Industries, we consider it our duty to keep Oregon's forests protected and sustained, for the future of our children and our children's children."

"And *their* children, too, I'll bet," added Doug. "And their children's children's children."

Katie nudged him and said, "How many beers have you had?"

Ned kept on smiling with those clear caramel eyes, and Holly did her best not to stare at the shred of steak.

"You ought to get Holly to tell you about her lip-reading," said Doug as they finished their raisin ice creams. "She's so good that she can even tell what part of the state a person was raised in."

"It's nothing," said Holly, embarrassed. "It's a knack, that's all."

"Doesn't sound like nothing to me," said Ned. He

leaned back in his chair and crossed his legs in his neatly pressed jeans. "Can you tell me what part of the state I was raised in?"

Holly hesitated but Doug said, "Go on, Holly. Tell him."

"I don't think so, really."

"Oh, come on," Ned coaxed her. "I've got twenty dollars that says you get it wrong."

Holly said, "Okay, it's a bet. Actually, you weren't raised in Oregon at all. Or at least your parents weren't."

"I wasn't?"

"No. Your accent is more like northeast Minnesota or northwest Wisconsin. Within a two-hundred-mile radius of Duluth, anyhow. Also, you twice used the word *sawbuck* when you were talking about cutting wood, whereas in Oregon they tend to use *buckstand* or *buckhorse*."

Ned turned to Doug and said, "Did you tell her that?"

Doug grinned and shook his head.

"You're sure? That is *amazing*. That is an absolutely amazing talent. My father started a lumber company in Babbitt, Minnesota, and I lived in Minnesota until I was seventeen. Then my father's company was taken over by North Minnesota Timber, and I was offered a job with Hood River. Amazing. And how did you know that stuff about sawbucks?"

"I make a study of it—you know, local and colloquial phrases. It helps me to tell where somebody's from and what kind of person they are. You know, white- or blue-collar, city or country."

"She does it for the Portland Police Bureau," said Doug proudly. "She's the only court-accredited lip-reader in Oregon."

Holly said, "Doug . . ." She didn't like anybody to know about her police work. Obviously she had been obliged to take Doug and Katie into her confidence, because of the erratic times that she needed to take off from the Children's Welfare Department. But for her own protection she didn't want murderers and drug dealers and sexual perverts finding out whose evidence it was that had sent them to jail.

But Doug plowed on. "Only yesterday she was lip-reading this guy who's going to have somebody's wife murdered. Can you believe that? There he was, in the Compass Hotel, arranging to have this woman killed like he's ordering lunch."

"That's amazing," said Ned. "You just don't realize what's going on all around you, do you, unless you know where to look."

"*Doug*," warned Holly. Then, to Ned, "You don't want to believe everything Doug says, especially after five beers."

"No, no, I haven't told you the best bit," said Doug. "The best bit is, this guy was talking about how they're going to dispose of this woman's body once they've killed her."

"Really? What were they going to do?"

"*Doug!*" snapped Holly, and Katie shook his arm and said, "For God's sake, Doug, it isn't funny."

"Of course it's funny. They're going to give the body to a guy they know in the wood-pulp business. The *wood-pulp* business! They're going to mush her up and turn her into cardboard boxes. So who's our number-one suspect?"

Doug slapped his thigh and let out a whoop of laughter. But then he realized that neither Holly, Katie, nor Ned was smiling at all, and his laughter petered out into a fit of coughing.

Ned said, in the flattest of voices, "Sorry, Doug. I know you were only kidding, but we at Hood River have total integrity when it comes to the raw materials we use in our mechanically ground-paper–making system. And what you call 'cardboard' boxes aren't made with cardboard at all; they're made with linerboard and corrugating medium, which is one hundred percent postconsumer recycled fiber."

Doug lifted both hands in surrender. "Okay, okay, I apologize. But when Holly told me about the wood-pulp guy, I have to admit that— Okay, sorry."

Back at the cabin they changed into warm coats and hiking boots so that they could take a walk up to Seven Arches Falls. Holly was ready first and came into the living room as Doug was poking the fire and building it up with more logs.

"Doug . . . I want you to know that I'm not angry with you or anything."

"I'm sorry, Holly. I opened my big yapola and stuck my foot straight into it, didn't I? But I think it's incredible, what you do. I just wanted Ned to know that we're proud of you."

"Doug, I have to think of my security. I have to think of Daisy as well as myself."

"I know that. But Ned . . . well, Katie and me, we've

known Ned almost as long as we've known each other."

"Do we ever get to know people, do you think? Like, *really* know them? I thought I knew David before I married him, and how wrong I was."

Doug stacked another log onto the hearth. "Let me tell you something: When you first walked into the Children's Welfare Department, my heart practically stopped on the spot. I had the biggest crush on you for months and months, until I realized that you weren't interested in me at all, and that I was never going to be able to summon up the courage to ask you out."

He turned to her, and there were tiny flames dancing in his eyes, like fireflies. "So . . . well, I accepted my lot, didn't I? I swallowed my disappointment. Katie's a really great girl, and I'm very fond of her. But I still look at you sometimes and wonder what it could have been like, you and me, and my heart still hurts, now and again, when I'm feeling sentimental, or drunk."

Holly reached out and held both his hands.

"I'm real sorry about spilling the beans," he said, swallowing hard. "It wasn't funny after all, was it, any of it?"

Holly said, "It doesn't matter, Doug. You're forgiven. But think about it: Supposing Ned *is* the wood-pulp guy?"

Cabin Fever

That night, unable to sleep, she stood with her forehead pressed against the chilly glass of her bedroom window, staring up at Mount Hood. The mountain appeared oddly insubstantial, almost fragile, as if it had been modeled out of nothing but crumpled white tissue paper.

She was very tired. During the afternoon they had climbed right up to the head of the Seven Arches Falls, so that they could see all seven separate cascades gushing down the mountainside into pool after foaming pool, and then down through the trees and the bushes to Mirror Lake. Then they had skirted the woods and descended an awkward rocky track, walking over five miles through the trees before coming back to the cabin.

Ned had stayed close to her side, offering his hand whenever she needed to climb up a slippery, moss-covered boulder, and even when she didn't. He had talked to her about thinning and sustained harvest and best management practices, and by the time they came through the cabin door she knew so much about forestry and wood products that she could have written a book about it—on recycled paper, of course.

After a supper of Katie's *chuletas veracruzana,* which were thick and spicy pork chops, they sat on the rug around the fireplace with glasses of pear brandy from the Clear Creek Distillery and told ghost stories.

Ned casually hung his arm around Holly's shoulders and made a point of turning to face her directly whenever he spoke, exaggerating his lip movements. He plainly believed that he was being considerate, but Holly could lip-read people who were stammering, and people who were muttering, and people who were talking so fast that even their friends told them to slow up, and after a while she began to find it wearing.

Katie told a story about when she was five years old, and had walked into the yard where her mother's washing was hanging out to dry. She said that she had seen a bas-relief figure appear in one of the sheets, a figure with a horrified face. But when the wind had suddenly flapped the sheet up in the air, she could see that there was nobody standing behind it, and she was alone.

Doug had glimpsed his dead father in the sporting-goods section of a Fred Meyer store. He had followed him from one aisle to another, trying to catch up with him, but his father had left the store and disappeared across the crowded parking lot. "One minute I could see him. . . . I knew it was him; he was even wearing his old felt hat. Next minute the sun dazzled me and it was just like he melted away."

Holly was about to tell them about seeing David's Porsche and what the woman in the bookstore had warned her about, but Ned got in first. "I never saw a ghost personally. I guess my upbringing was too rational, ha-ha. But up in the woods of Minnesota they have this story about a shadow that attacks people at night. It comes out of the woods and it grabs you by your hair, and then it drags you back into the forest and nobody ever sees you again, ever."

She picked up her wristwatch from her night table. Ten after two. She supposed she ought to try to sleep, but for some reason she felt disturbed, as if something were badly wrong. She looked toward the oil painting of the woman in the field and she almost expected the black bird to fly off the post and flap off into the painted sky.

After a while she returned to bed and pulled the blankets up to her neck. She wished she hadn't come here to Mirror Lake, and that she was back in her apartment, with Daisy and all her Barbies sleeping in the next bedroom. It was not that she particularly disliked Ned. It was just that she didn't find him at all interesting—or wood pulp, for that matter—and yet, he had demanded so much of her attention. Even when she had taken her drink out onto the veranda late that evening, just to smell the pines, he had followed her and stood uncomfortably close to her and given her a *Reader's Digest*–style exposition about the magic of the forest and how his heart was at one with the wilderness. She hadn't even been able to turn her back on him, because he would have known immediately that she wasn't listening.

• • •

She was actually asleep and dreaming about walking in the darkest reaches of the forest when she was woken up by somebody lifting the blankets behind her. Immediately she turned around, and as she did so Ned climbed naked into bed with her and put his arms around her. He was hairy-chested and hairy-thighed, and she felt his erection bump against her hip.

"*Get out!*" she shouted at him. *"What the hell do you think you're doing? Get the hell out of my bed!"*

He tried to pull her even closer, tugging up her nightshirt, but she twisted herself around, kicked at him with her heels, and climbed right out of bed. She switched on the bedside lamp and he was sitting up blinking at her, and he was actually *grinning*.

"Get out," she told him. She said it more quietly now, because she didn't want her voice to sound shrill and out of control. "I don't know what gave you the idea that I was the slightest bit interested in you, but believe me, I'm not."

"Well, *that's* real hard to figure," he said, without the slightest trace of embarrassment. "From the way you've been coming on to me all day, I definitely got the impression that you were more than ready for a bit of grown-up playtime."

"Just get out."

"Hey, steady, Holly. There's no call to be so unfriendly."

"Do you want me to call Doug and have him throw you out?"

"Doug? *Doug?* I hope you're not serious."

Holly walked around the bed and threw open the door. Ned said, *"Pfff,"* and slowly shook his head, as if he couldn't believe that she really wanted him to go. "You know what Doug told me about you? Doug said that you were a real fun girl."

"I'll tell you how fun I am. I'm fun enough to call the police and make a complaint of attempted rape."

"Well, excuse me. Somebody with a disability like yours, I thought they would have jumped at the chance to have a good time with a good-looking guy."

"I'm deaf, Ned. I'm not a leper. Now go."

"Okeydokey. Your loss. But don't you try making any trouble."

"What do you mean?"

"I mean that Doug and Katie both saw how much you'd taken a shine to me today, and if I was to tell them that you'd come on to me . . ."

He climbed out of bed and came right up to her. He was reeking of sweat and alcohol, as if he had been drinking and masturbating to work himself up to invading her bedroom, and his penis was slowly sinking. He looked her in the eyes and said, "If I was to say that *you* came into *my* room, just begging for it, and I'd behaved like a gentleman and sent you away and that you were just trying to be vengeful . . . well, Doug and Katie and me, we've all known each other a very long time. We're like *family*. Who do you think they'd believe?"

He stood only inches away from her, swaying. "Am I speaking *s-l-o-w* enough for you? You do *u-n-d-e-r-s-t-a-n-d* me, don't you?"

"Get out," she repeated.

"Okay . . . have it your way. But I'll tell you this: I never realized that being deaf lowered your sex drive. You learn something every day."

He lurched out of the room and she turned away so that she wouldn't have to look at his backside. She closed the door behind him and locked it. Her heart was thumping against her ribs as though somebody were knocking a tennis ball against a wall. She sat down on the foot of the bed, her hands clasped tightly together. She felt like crying but she was braver than that, and in any case she couldn't find any tears.

Holly Tells a Lie

"Sorry that your daughter's sick," said Ned, smiling, one hand raised to shield his eyes from the morning sunshine. "Hope she gets better real quick."

Holly stood by while Doug lifted her weekend case into the back of the Voyager. Katie came up and gave her a hug and a kiss and said, "Give Daisy our love, won't you? I'm sure she's going to be okay." Holly climbed into the front passenger seat and Doug shut the door.

They drove back toward the main highway with the sunshine flickering between the trees like a zoetrope. After a while Doug said, "Everything's *okay*, isn't it? I mean, between you and us."

"Sure, everything's fine. I'm worried about Daisy, that's all."

"Well, of course you are. What happened to you when you were young—I guess it tends to make you doubly anxious anytime Daisy runs a fever."

They reached Interstate 84 and headed back toward Portland. "I'm sorry I spoiled your weekend," said Holly.

"Hey, don't even think about it. I'll be back at the lake by twelve. Plenty of time to get some fishing in.

He offered her some gum, but she shook her head. He folded a stick into his mouth and said, "Ned's a great guy, isn't he?"

Holly told a lie.

A Weekend Alone

She spent the rest of the weekend alone, reading, watching television, varnishing her nails, eating pasta from the restaurant downstairs.

Now and then she went to the window and looked down into the street below. Once or twice she thought she could see a black, shadowy figure underneath the awning of the map and antique print shop on the opposite corner, but she was never sure if it was a figure or just a shadow. Sometimes it looked tall and jagged. At other times it flapped, like a dark overcoat blowing in the wind.

On Sunday afternoon she came across a quotation in the arts section of *The Oregonian*, a poem by P. J. Quint. It read, "*Inside my cupboard I heard people talk, and laugh / Were they discussing me? I could not clearly hear / And so I stood, as minutes of my life went by / Listening in indecision, and in fear.*" For some reason she found this poem deeply disturbing and didn't want to go into the kitchen after that, or open a cupboard door.

That evening she went to bed early and treated herself to fresh pearl-colored nail polish, a bright green Lancôme face mask, and a bikini-line depilatory cream that smelled like burning carpet. After she had showered, she went to her bedroom window and looked out over the street. The lights of the city glittered in the evening wind. She saw three men arguing on the corner. One of them kept going away and coming back again, jabbing his finger in anger. She saw a woman hurrying along the sidewalk. The woman kept turning to look behind her as if she were being pursued. Her shadow looked like the shadow of a giant bird's wing.

The Doctor Is In

Holly had just taken a mouthful of sprinkled doughnut when Emma signaled to her from the switchboard. She went out into the reception area, sucking her fingers.

"Dr. Ferdinand, from East Portland Memorial," said Emma.

"Oh, great. You've told him that I can't speak to him in person?"

Emma nodded and said, "She's right here, Dr. Ferdinand. Yes, she says good morning to you, too, and thank you for calling back."

Holly said, "Ask him about Casper Beale."

"Oh, yes," said Emma. "Ms. Summers is interested in a patient of yours, Casper Beale?"

There was a pause, and then Emma turned back to Holly. "He doesn't have any patients of that name."

"A boy. An eleven-year-old boy, with non-Hodgkin's lymphoma."

"No, sorry."

"Is he sure about that? His parents are separated, so maybe he's registered under another name."

"He doesn't have *any* eleven-year-old boys with non-Hodgkin's lymphoma. Nor eleven-year-old girls, either."

"But tell him I've met Casper Beale myself. He lives with his mother on Southeast Boise. They had an appeal for him in the media. His neighbors raised money last fall to send him to Disneyland."

"No. Sorry. Positively not."

When Emma had hung up, Holly stood beside her for two or three minutes, thinking. If Casper Beale wasn't a patient of Dr. Ferdinand's, then whose patient was he?

"Emma . . . if I make you a list of hospitals with pediatric cancer units, would you call them for me and ask if they have Casper Beale on their lists?"

"Sure thing. What happens if they don't?"

"I don't know. I don't even want to think about it."

Suspicion

It was foggy when she arrived at the Heilshorn house early that afternoon. It was that dead-cold Portland fog that turns the city's eastern suburbs into a silent community of ghost houses, with ghostly cars rolling along the streets and ghostly children playing on the sidewalks.

The garage door was open so that she could see a Dodge station wagon parked inside, and there was a black late-model Lincoln Town Car parked in the driveway behind it.

She rang the bell and almost immediately a middle-aged man opened the front door. He was medium height, almost bald, with a plump, well-fed face and a cast in his eyes, so that his left eye appeared to be looking over Holly's right shoulder. He wore a white business shirt and black pants and checkered argyle socks.

"Mr. Heilshorn?" asked Holly, producing her ID card. "I expect your wife's told you that we have an appointment."

"That's the reason I'm here," said Mr. Heilshorn

sharply. "I can't say that I'm anything but outraged at what's being implied here, but I wanted to tell you face-to-face that this is a family with nothing to hide."

"Do you mind if I come in?"

He stepped back to allow her into the hallway. "Your, uh, footwear, please?" he said, nodding down toward her feet. "New carpet. My wife likes to keep things pretty much immaculate."

"Yes. She said that before."

Holly took off her brogues and Mr. Heilshorn led her into the living room. Mrs. Heilshorn was already posed in an armchair next to the fireplace, dressed in a yellow satin catsuit with a deep décolletage, a matching yellow scarf tied around her hair. Beside her, on the arm of the chair, sat a pale, pretty little girl with brown bobbed hair and big brown eyes, wearing a pink sweat-shirt and a stonewashed denim skirt.

"Hello again, Mrs. Heilshorn," said Holly. "So this is Sarah-Jane."

"Sarah-Jane can confirm that she got her bruises from her bicycle," said Mrs. Heilshorn, without waiting to be prompted.

Holly sat down and propped her notepad on her knees. "Sarah-Jane, my name is Holly and it's my job to take care of children when they get hurt."

"Sarah-Jane got her bruises from her bicycle, didn't you, Sarah-Jane?"

"Mrs. Heilshorn, I'm sure that there's no serious problem here, but I'm directed by state legislation to investigate. I'm sure you understand why."

"Listen," said Mr. Heilshorn, "we're a respectable, law-abiding family. I pay my taxes, I work for Oregon-

Pacific Realty. My company donated a fountain to the art museum."

"All the same, Mr. Heilshorn, we were alerted by Sarah-Jane's school and I'm sure that you can understand why we have to look into the matter."

"I *don't,* as a matter of fact. You're virtually accusing me of—"

Holly waited. Mr. Heilshorn spun his hand around in his effort to explain himself.

"Well, what you're implying here, I wouldn't even *say* it in front of Sarah-Jane, let alone think of— Jesus, she wouldn't even know what I was talking about."

Holly took out her pen. "There's no accusation here, Mr. Heilshorn. But if you're agreeable, I'd like to talk to Sarah-Jane alone for just a few minutes. I'm sure that we can clear this up without any need for acrimony."

"Acrimony? Jesus. This is my ten-year-old daughter here."

"I know, Mr. Heilshorn. But if you can give me five minutes alone with her . . ."

Mr. Heilshorn shoved his hands into his pockets and took a deep, flaring breath. "All right," he said, at last. "All right, fine. You can talk to her alone. But believe me, you're wasting your time. I can tell you right now what she's going to say. She's going to say that she slipped off her bicycle seat and that's all there is to it."

It was then that he took hold of Sarah-Jane's hand and squeezed it so tight that her knuckles were spotted with white.

"That's what you're going to tell the lady, aren't you, sugar?"

Sarah-Jane looked up at him and gave him the

briefest of smiles and nodded. But Holly saw something in her eyes, and it wasn't the panic that she had
seen in Mrs. Heilshorn's: It was weariness. Sexual
abuse, in the end, always makes children weary.

"So . . . your mom tells me you're out on your bike a
whole lot."

Sarah-Jane nodded.

"She says every day and sometimes she doesn't even
know where you go."

"I always tell her. I only go to see Kylie in Tabor
Vista. And my friend Penny sometimes, but she lives all
the way down on Division."

"I see. Do you have any boyfriends?"

Sarah-Jane blushed and shook her head.

"Not even one boy you like?"

"Well, Kylie's brother Lennie, but he's just her
brother."

"Does Lennie like you?"

"I guess. He talks to me sometimes but that's all."

"How old is Lennie?"

"Sixteen, I think. But he doesn't act like he's sixteen.
I mean, he's nice to me."

"Did he ever kiss you?"

Sarah-Jane burst out into frantic giggling. *"No!* No,
never!"

"Did he ever touch you at all?"

"Uh-uh."

"He didn't touch you in any way that could have
caused those bruises on your legs?"

Sarah-Jane looked serious. "He never touched me,
ever."

"Did anybody else ever touch you in a way that could have caused those bruises on your legs?"

Sarah-Jane shook her head again. Holly could sense her extreme tension. She began to knock her knees together as if she needed to go to the bathroom, and bite at her left-hand fingernails, and kept clearing her throat in little high-pitched hiccups.

"Your daddy and mommy say that those bruises on your legs were caused by your bicycle seat. Do you want to tell me how exactly that happens?"

"I guess I jump off the seat too quick when I stop."

"But how do you get bruised by the seat if you've already jumped off it?"

"I don't know. I just do. It happens all the time."

"Do you mind if I look at your bruises?"

Sarah-Jane hesitated and then she said, "Okay." She lifted her skirt two or three inches. Holly saw a pattern of bruises about the size and shape of large black grapes. Some of them had faded to yellow, but there were others that were clearly more recent.

"Okay, that's fine. Thank you. When was the last time you bruised yourself?"

"Yesterday," Sarah-Jane whispered unhappily.

"Well, I have to tell you, honey, I saw your bicycle and it has a big soft seat, and I'm finding it very difficult to believe that all of those bruises could have been caused just by your hopping on and off it. Do you know what those bruises look like to me?"

"No."

"They look to me like somebody's been grabbing hold of you . . . somebody strong. Do you think that could have happened? Because—let me tell you now—nobody's going to be angry with you if that's what really happened. It wasn't your fault, not your fault at all. But it's very important that we find out where those bruises came from, because we don't want you to get any more. Even if it means the state of Oregon buying you a brand-new bicycle, one that doesn't hurt you like this."

Sarah-Jane lowered her head and twisted her plastic-bead bracelet around and around. Holly waited without saying anything while the mock-rococo clock on the mantelpiece crept slowly past four, and although she couldn't hear it, she could guess that it marked the moment with a fancy little chime.

Holly reached out and took hold of Sarah-Jane's hand. "You don't have to suffer this anymore, Sarah-Jane. All you have to do is tell me what really happened and I can make sure that it never happens again. Ever."

Tears began to slide down Sarah-Jane's cheeks. She said miserably, "It was my bicycle seat," and then she covered her face with her hands, and Holly couldn't even persuade her to look up at her, let alone say any more.

Tragedy

"**M**r. and Mrs. Heilshorn, I have to tell you that my strong suspicion is that Sarah-Jane has been physically abused. More than likely by an adult, judging by the size and the span of the fingermarks."

Mr. Heilshorn's left eye glared furiously over her shoulder. "Do you know what you're saying here?" he demanded.

"Absolutely. The school doctor suspected it, and now that I've had the opportunity to talk to Sarah-Jane for myself, I'm convinced of it."

"On what fucking grounds, may I ask?"

"Mr. Heilshorn, there's no need to be abusive. I'm just doing my job, which is protecting vulnerable children like your daughter from physical and emotional harm."

"You're trying to accuse me of precisely what?"

"I'm not accusing you of anything, Mr. Heilshorn. It's not my job to accuse you of anything. My job is simply to assess Sarah-Jane's situation here and if necessary to recommend further investigation into her physical and emotional well-being. Which I'm telling you now is what I intend to do."

"She never gets sick," Mrs. Heilshorn put in. "I give her an excellent diet, the same as me. Plenty of fruit, plenty of vegetables."

"Mrs. Heilshorn, we're not discussing what Sarah-Jane has for lunch. We're talking about the possibility that somebody has sexually abused her."

"From a few fucking bruises? What do they prove? Sarah-Jane and me, we often have a rough-and-tumble. You know, horsing around in the yard, stuff like that. Sometimes I give her piggybacks—so what? I'm her father, for Christ's sake."

Mrs. Heilshorn said nothing but gnawed at her bright scarlet lips and looked anxious.

Holly put her notes away. "I'm going to recommend that you bring Sarah-Jane into the children's clinic for examination by a police doctor. If she really did sustain those bruises from falling off her bicycle seat and horsing around in the yard, we'll soon be able to tell for sure. I can make an appointment now."

"She's a virgin," Mr. Heilshorn interrupted. "I can absolutely guarantee that, one hundred and ten percent."

"Well, as I say, we'll soon be able to confirm it."

"Jesus, I don't believe this. I don't believe that you can walk into my home and suggest that I— Jesus. I mean, what kind of people are you? You got dirty minds or what?"

Holly stood up. "I'm sorry, Mr. Heilshorn. I'm doing my job, that's all. Why don't you bring Sarah-Jane along to the clinic tomorrow morning and we can put this matter to rest."

"I'm going to call my lawyer, I warn you. I'm going to sue you for slander and invasion of my personal privacy."

"Somebody's personal privacy may have been invaded here, Mr. Heilshorn, but I certainly don't think it's yours. Now, do you mind if I have another quick word with Sarah-Jane before I leave? I want to tell her what's going to happen tomorrow."

Mrs. Heilshorn said, "I'll get her," and left the living room. Mr. Heilshorn said nothing but glowered at Holly and intermittently sniffed. Holly used her cell phone to text the clinic and arrange for Sarah-Jane's examination.

"Eleven forty-five okay for you?" she asked Mr. Heilshorn. He gave her a dismissive wave of his hand.

It was then that Mrs. Heilshorn came back in, looking flustered. "She's locked herself in her room and she won't answer when I knock."

"I'm not fucking surprised. You think she's stupid? She knows what's going on here. Trying to say that I molested my own daughter . . . Jesus."

"Her appointment's at eleven forty-five," Holly told Mrs. Heilshorn. "Can you make sure that she's there on time? Here's the address, and here's my cell phone number in case you need me."

Mr. Heilshorn snatched her visiting card and peered at it. "Holly Summers. Well, I can't say that it's been much of a pleasure to meet you, Ms. Summers. Goodbye."

"I still need to have a word with Sarah-Jane before I go."

"And what if I say you can't?"

"Then I'll have to call the police and I'm sure you don't want a squad car in the street outside your home."

"I'll try knocking again," said Mrs. Heilshorn.

"Jesus."

Holly followed Mrs. Heilshorn up the blue-shag-carpeted stairs to the second-story landing. She tip-toed across to a door with a flowery ceramic plaque saying *Sarah-Jane's Palace* and gave a brisk little rap. "Sarah-Jane? Sarah-Jane? It's Mommy again. Can you open the door, please?"

There was no answer. She tried rapping again. "Sarah-Jane, I don't want to have to get cross with you!"

Holly said, "Let me try." She leaned close to the door and said, "Sarah-Jane. This is Holly. I need to tell you something important before I go back to the office. It'll help you to understand what's going to happen tomorrow."

She paused and then she said, "I know this is difficult for you, but you're very grown-up and I know that you can get through it. Do you think you could come out and talk?"

Still no answer. Mrs. Heilshorn looked at Holly and shrugged. "She can be very sulky when she wants to be. You know what they're like at this age."

"I think we ought to open the door," said Holly.

"But she's locked it."

"I still think we ought to open it. Can you ask your husband to come up here and help us?"

"Anthony, will you come upstairs, please? Ms. Summers thinks we ought to open the door."

"Jesus."

But after Holly and Mrs. Heilshorn had knocked again and again, still with no reply, he came stamping up the stairs and beat on the door himself. "Sarah-Jane! Will you stop acting so goddamn childish! Open the goddamn door!"

Silence. Mr. Heilshorn turned to Holly and pointed a finger at her. "If I break this door down, I want the city to pay for it, you got me?"

"Please, Mr. Heilshorn. Just open the door."

He gripped the frame in both hands and gave the door one hefty kick with his stockinged foot, and then another. The door splintered around the lock, and a shove with his shoulder was enough to open it.

Inside, Sarah-Jane's Palace was as neat and as perfect as Mrs. Heilshorn's Palace downstairs. A brass-knobbed bed with a pink satin quilt. A white dressing table with ruched lace skirts around it, and a silver-backed comb-and-brush set. Heaps of teddy bears and floppy-eared bunnies and frogs. Posters of pop stars.

"So where is she?" Mr. Heilshorn wanted to know.

"She has to be here. She locked the door from the inside. Unless she climbed out the window."

Mr. Heilshorn went to the window. "She couldn't have. The window's locked from the inside too." Grunting, he bent over and peered under the bed. "No, not there. . . . So where the hell is she?"

Holly opened the closet door. Inside, on a high brass rail, hung color-coordinated coats and dresses and slacks, all perfectly pressed, and these had been pushed along to one side so that Sarah-Jane could knot a white rope belt around her neck and hang herself. She had used a little red-roofed Fisher-Price dollhouse to stand on, kicking it over onto its side. Her eyes bulged out in a furious stare, and her lips were turquoise. She resembled a grotesque puppet from *Sesame Street,* rather than the pretty little girl whom Holly had talked with downstairs.

Mrs. Heilshorn let out a terrible shriek, more like a war whoop, and dropped onto the bed with her red-clawed hand held over her mouth. Mr. Heilshorn immediately rushed into the closet and seized Sarah-Jane around the hips to take her weight. *"Untie her!"* he screamed. *"Untie her!"*

Later, Mrs. Heilshorn came downstairs, her mascara blotched, her yellow scarf looped untidily on one side. She came up to Holly and handed her a piece of paper that looked as if it had been torn from a school exercise book.

"I suppose the police better see this."

Holly took it. A short message was scrawled, hurriedly, in purple crayon. It said, *It wasn't daddys fault it was my fault love sarahjane.*

Detective Sergeant Gene Brushmore: So what was it that wasn't your fault?

Anthony Heilshorn: I don't know what she meant. Maybe she was worried about the bruises, the accusation that was being made.

Brushmore: You mean the suspicion that she was being sexually abused.

Roger T. Floren, Attorney: My client utterly refutes this suggestion and we will be showing that it was made recklessly and willfully by the Hawthorne School doctor and by Ms. Holly Summers from the Portland Children's Welfare Department, and in effect they were indirectly responsible for Sarah-Jane taking her own life.

Brushmore: The medical examiner . . . in his preliminary medical examination . . . the ME says that there is absolutely no question that Sarah-Jane had been sexually . . . you know, sexually interfered with. Molested.

Floren: Even if this is true, my client denies that he was responsible.

Heilshorn: I loved her. You think I would have . . . ? I wouldn't. I couldn't.

3:54 A.M.

Brushmore: [Coughs.] Detective Janet Spectorsky has been talking to your wife, Mr. Heilshorn, and your wife has made a statement of her own free will that you regularly took Sarah-Jane into the roll-out bed in your—what you called your "Lion's Den." And this was done for sexual purposes.

Floren: Come on, Sergeant. You can't expect my client to respond to an allegation like that.

Heilshorn: Wait a minute here. You don't see it for what it was, do you? You just don't see it. There was no— Valerie and me hadn't had any kind of a marriage since Sarah-Jane was born. It was like she totally lost interest in the physical side of things. She never allowed me to touch her; she never even allowed me to *look* at her, for Christ's sake. She's my wife, but I haven't seen her undressed in over ten years. Glimpses, but what's glimpses?

Brushmore: So the arrangement seems to have been that you had sex with Sarah-Jane instead? And your wife allowed it? Encouraged it, even, so that she wouldn't have to have sex with you herself?

Floren: My client isn't saying that at all. Come on,

Anthony, you don't have to answer any more questions. It's nearly four in the morning, we're all . . . This is putting my client under duress.

Heilshorn: I loved her. I was very careful. I tried my best not to hurt her.

Floren: Anthony, you don't have to say any of this.

Heilshorn: [Beginning to weep.] You don't see it, do you? I loved her.

Brushmore: She was your daughter, Mr. Heilshorn. She was only ten and a half years old, and you were regularly having full, penetrative sex with her.

Heilshorn: She was still a virgin. I never did that to her. I swear to God that she was still a virgin.

Brushmore: What are you trying to say to me here? Your wife says that she frequently found blood and other stains on your sheets. Here it is: "I had to strip the bed and wash the sheets at least twice every week. . . . I like everything perfect."

Floren: That's enough, Sergeant. This interview concludes now.

Heilshorn: What does it matter? She's dead.

Floren: It matters, Anthony, because you have a constitutional right not to incriminate yourself.

Heilshorn: She's dead! Okay? I had sex with her, yes. Played with her. Made love to her. We called it "playing lions and tigers," I don't really know why. I went into her, yes, but I was her father, and I took that responsibility seriously, and that's why I never took her virginity.

Brushmore: You're saying that—?

Heilshorn: Yes, her bottom. Her little tush, we called it.

Brushmore: You anally penetrated your own daughter at least twice a week and you're trying to tell me that this was the behavior of a caring and responsible father?

Floren: [Throws down pencil.] God give me strength.

Heilshorn: You don't see it, do you? I *loved* her, and she loved me.

Hugging Daisy

After Marcella had cleaned up the kitchen and gone home, Holly sat on the couch with Daisy and hugged her. Daisy always knew when she had seen something terrible at work, because she brushed her hair for her and kissed her and looked at her as if she could never look at her enough. It was warm in the apartment and still smelled of Marcella's bean stew, and Holly played "Have I Told You Lately That I Love You?" at least six times. She couldn't hear it herself, of course, but it was Daisy's favorite.

When Daisy was asleep, Holly went into her room and looked at her some more, as if all this looking could erase the vision of Sarah-Jane hanging in her clothes closet. But the pain of thinking about Sarah-Jane's suffering was more than she could bear, and after a while she had to close Daisy's door and stand in the corridor outside with tears running down her cheeks and her mouth puckered to stop herself from sobbing.

She knew now what she would do with the Cinderella doll that Mickey had given her. After Sarah-Jane's funeral, she would go and lay it on her grave.

A Sour Morning

Doug called her into his office as soon as she arrived at work. He was standing by the window with his hands in his pockets, and even when she came in he didn't look around.

"Doug?" she said at last.

He turned to face her. "That Heilshorn business: We're going to be crucified."

"What else did you expect me to do? I discussed it with you Thursday. There was nothing to indicate that urgent action was called for, and in any case I don't think that time was the factor here."

"I'm afraid the press don't see it that way. Did you see the TV news this morning? Have you read the papers?"

"I haven't had time, Doug. I had to get Daisy off to school."

Doug slapped a copy of *The Oregonian* down on his desk. "Here it is: *Portland Children's Welfare Department in State of Paralysis. Children at Risk Being Sacrificed by Over-Cautious Caseworkers.* Too little, too late. Daniel Joseph one week, Sarah-Jane Heilshorn the next."

"For God's sake, Doug, you know how difficult it is to assess any abuse. The parents are devious; the kids are too confused or intimidated to say anything. Or they have their moral compass completely screwed up, like Sarah-Jane."

"Holly, it's your job to stop these things happening before they happen. You're deaf, I'll grant you that. But when children's lives are at stake, I can't make any concessions."

"My deafness has nothing to do with this. I discussed the Heilshorn case with you Thursday and you agreed that it was safer to leave it until Monday."

"You were in the damn house when the girl hung herself! You were actually *there!* Have you seen what it says here in the paper? 'Caseworker Holly Summers is stone deaf, and it is a tribute to her personal courage that she has overcome this handicap to help children in need. But in this case she wasn't only deaf but blind, too, and an innocent little girl lost her life.' The director is furious."

Holly waited while Doug took his glasses on and off, rubbed the back of his neck, and rearranged the papers on his desk. "So what do you want me to do?" she asked at last.

"I don't want you to do anything."

"I was going to go see the Pfeiffer family this morning, over on Tiggetts Southeast."

"Helen will do that for you."

"Meaning what?"

"Meaning that Helen will do that for you: You're suspended."

"Suspended? Doug, what on earth are you talking

about? I can't be suspended: I have a full caseload this week, and next week's even worse."

Doug stared at her and she couldn't even be sure that it was really him. He was more like Doug taken over by *The Bodysnatchers*. "Sorry, that's the decision."

"So what's going to happen to Daniel Joseph? And who's going to give the expert assessment in the Heilshorn case?"

Doug kept his eyes lowered but he said, "Not you, that's for sure. We can't take the risk. If a court holds the city liable for what happened to Daniel Joseph or Sarah-Jane Heilshorn, we could be looking at compensation that runs into tens of millions of dollars."

"So how long is this suspension going to last, if you don't mind my asking?"

"I don't know . . . at least until these two cases have been cleared up."

"I see. So what do you expect me to do now, go home and play solitaire?"

Doug shrugged. "I'm sorry. That's all I can say. *My* job's on the line too."

"All right. You have my number if you need me. Maybe we can talk about this later, out of office hours, as friends."

"Well, ah, there's something else I wanted to say. Not related to work."

"Yes?"

"It's difficult to know how to put this, but Saturday night, up at the cabin . . ."

"Yes, go on. What?"

"You weren't entirely truthful about the reason you left so suddenly, were you?"

Holly stared at him. She couldn't work out what this was leading up to, but Doug was obviously very uncomfortable about what he was going to say next.

"The thing of it is, Holly, Ned told us in confidence about your going into his room."

"Ned said *what?*"

"He was very embarrassed. Didn't really want to mention it at all. But he thought we ought to know about it, in case . . . well, in case we ever invited you to Mirror Lake again, with some other man who might not be so laid-back about it."

Holly could feel her cheeks flushing. "*Laid-back?* Do you want to know what really happened that night?"

"Holly, I really don't want to discuss this any further. I think we have enough departmental difficulty here without getting involved in any personal unpleasantness."

"No, wait up, Doug. Let me get this straight. You and Katie really believe that I tried to *seduce* that bozo?"

"Ned's been a very dear friend of ours for years, Holly. He's as straight as an arrow."

"So what am I?"

Doug was about to answer when his phone flashed. He picked it up and said, "Yes. Yes, Mike, I've told her. Well, of course she's not happy about it. None of us are happy about it. At ten? Okay. And, Mike, I just want to say again how sorry I am. We all are. The whole department."

He put down the phone. "Mike Pulaski."

"I gathered."

"We're having a damage limitation meeting at ten. See what we can do to—"

"—limit the damage?"

Doug nodded.

Holly took out her ID card and tossed it onto his desk. "The damage is already done, Doug. You haven't had the guts to support me in either of these cases, and on top of that, you have the barefaced nerve to accuse me of acting like a slut. If this is the kind of man you are, I'm very, very glad to be suspended. In fact, I quit."

"Holly—"

"What?" she challenged him.

"Nothing. I'm sorry it had to turn out like this, that's all."

As she was clearing out her desk drawer, Emma came in.

"What's happening?" she asked, wide-eyed.

"I quit. I'm leaving. I've had enough."

"Really?"

"Really. It's this Heilshorn case. Well, the Joseph case too. Doug's going to throw me to the wolves."

"I can't say that I'm surprised. I overheard them talking this morning and Doug was saying something about a sacrificial lamb."

"That's right, *me*."

"They'll ask you back, you know," said Emma, sitting on the edge of her desk. "They can't run the Children's Welfare Department without you."

Holly shook her head. "I wouldn't come back if Doug Yeats crawled into the room stark naked with *SORRY* written on his ass and kissed my feet."

"Yuck, neither would I."

Holly reached over and picked a ballpoint pen out of her jelly jar. "Here: Write down your cell phone number. I don't want to lose touch."

She cleared out the last of her desk. She found a very old packet of Jelly Bellies in the back of her drawer, so old that they had all turned crusty-white. She dropped them into the wastebasket along with her Japanese Garden calendar and a plaster statuette of Little Orphan Annie that Doug had given her. "By the way, did you find out where Casper Beale is being treated?"

"No," said Emma. "I was going to tell you about that. I called every cancer unit in the Portland area and none of them had anybody called Casper Beale on their records. So I looked up the Casper Beale Cancer Fund on the Internet. There was a story about it in the *Portland Tribune* on October 17 last year. According to that, Casper was being treated at the Tasco Clinic in Seattle, which has a very highly specialized unit for treating children with cancer."

"And?"

"The Tasco Clinic had never heard of him, either. Or anyone like him."

Charity Begins at Home

Late that afternoon, she drove back across the Ross Island Bridge to Southeast Boise. This time there was no Mrs. Beale outside in the driveway, washing her brand-new Malibu, or overweight children playing on the sidewalk. In fact, the entire street was deserted, except for a mangy orange dog and the ripped-up pages of an *Incredible Hulk* comic scattering in the wind.

She rang the doorbell. She hoped that it worked, because she had no way of telling. She waited but there was no answer. She cupped her hands around her face and peered in through the yellow glass window beside the door. She was sure she could see somebody moving around inside. She rapped on the glass with her keys and shouted out, "Mrs. Beale? Mrs. Beale? Can you open the door, please?"

Almost a minute went past and then the door was opened, only five or six inches. She could see Mrs. Beale in a white satin bathrobe covered in splashy scarlet poppies, like August Moon's blood-spattered shirt at the Chinese supermarket. A cigarette was hanging from between Mrs. Beale's lips, so that one of her puffy eyes was closed against the smoke. It looked as if she were giving Holly a long, knowing wink.

"It's you again. What the hell do you want? I thought I told you to leave me the hell alone."

She was about to close the door but Holly quickly pushed her hand against it to keep it open. What she was about to do was in blatant disregard of department regulations. But then she thought, *I've quit. They can't fire me now that I've quit. Besides, I'm doing this for Casper, not the Children's Welfare Department. I'm doing this for me and Casper and nobody else.*

"Mrs. Beale," she said, "I'm pretty sure I've found out what you've been doing." Her voice was strangled and off-key, although she couldn't hear it.

"What the hell do you mean? Get out of here."

"You haven't been taking Casper to the Tasco Clinic, have you? Or any other hospital?"

"What?"

"Casper doesn't have cancer, does he? In fact, there's nothing wrong with him at all."

Mrs. Beale slowly took the cigarette out of her mouth and blew smoke. "I don't know what you're talking about. What the hell are you talking about?"

"I'm talking about the Casper Beale Cancer Fund. You bought yourself a new car and a plasma-screen TV and you took yourself off to a vacation at Disneyland. Thirty-five thousand dollars' worth, at least."

Mrs. Beale opened the door wider. "You listen to me, lady. Casper's sick. You spoke to him yourself. He's dying. He *needs* those things."

UNSPEAKABLE215

"He doesn't need anything, Mrs. Beale, except love, and feeding, and proper care."

"You're trying to suggest what? Interfering do-gooders like you—that's so typical. You'd deny a dying boy a decent TV? He can't play in the street, he can't go to school, he can't go swimming. He can hardly walk. What else can he do but watch TV?"

"I'm not talking about TV, Mrs. Beale. I'm talking about systematic child abuse. You've been starving him on purpose, to make him look as if he's sick."

As she spoke, Casper appeared in the hallway behind her. He was wearing the same faded red pajamas that he had been wearing the last time Holly saw him. He looked infinitely old, and he walked with a slow, hesitant shuffle.

"Momma," he said.

Mrs. Beale didn't even turn around. "Casper, go back to your room!"

"I feel pukey," said Casper tiredly.

"Go to the bathroom if you feel pukey. Don't bother me now."

To Holly, she said, "And you. You can get the hell out of here and leave me alone, before I call a cop."

"You won't do that," said Holly.

"Oh, no?"

"You won't do that because you know that you're guilty of willful mistreatment. Casper, listen to me. Do you know what your momma's been doing? You don't have cancer at all. You never have."

Casper slowly raised his eyes toward his mother and blinked in bewilderment. Mrs. Beale wrapped her robe even more tightly around her bosom and said, "You're crazy, you know that? Of *course* he has cancer. Non-Hodgkin's lymphoma. Look at him."

"Any child would look like that if you half-starved him and shaved his head and gave him stuff to make him vomit if he ever looked like he was putting on weight."

"You'd better watch what you're saying! You don't have any idea what I've had to go through, ever since he got sick. I've never slept more than two hours a night. I've been cleaning up puke and changing his sheets for nearly two years, and what am I going to get at the end of it? A broken heart, that's all."

"Oh, you might squeeze in one more vacation to Disneyland," said Holly. "I'll bet you didn't even take Casper along with you, did you, the last time you went? What did you do, leave him at home to fend for himself?"

"I needed it!" Mrs. Beale screamed at her. "I needed that vacation! I deserved it!"

Casper weakly sat down on the doormat. Holly opened up her bag and took out a folded printout of a newspaper story.

"Two and a half years ago, Mrs. Beale. A story on the back page of *The Oregonian*. A woman in San Antonio, Texas, pretended that her daughter had cancer. She fed her on nothing but Cream of Wheat with sour milk and sleeping pills, and she shaved her head to make it look as if she were undergoing chemotherapy. She went to the library and took out books on leukemia so that she would know what she was talking about. She even arranged for the girl to have psychiatric counseling, to prepare her for an early death."

Mrs. Beale looked confused. She kept shaking her head and furiously scratching her elbow, but she didn't seem to be able to speak.

Holly shook the printout at her. "Do you know what she did, this woman in San Antonio? She and her neighbors organized fund-raisers to pay for the little girl to have specialist cancer treatment, and a vacation in Florida, and all kinds of goodies.

"But of course she *didn't* die because she didn't have cancer at all, any more than Casper has cancer. You saw this story, didn't you, and you thought to yourself: *If this woman can do it, so can I.* Except that you made sure that Casper looked really, really sick, so you wouldn't get found out, the way that this woman was. She forgot to shave her daughter's head one day, but *you* never forgot, did you? You've ruined Casper—ruined him for the rest of his life, probably. Physically and mentally. And for what? Ten days in Disneyland and a TV and a car."

Mrs. Beale muttered, "He's sick. You can see that he's sick." But she seemed incapable of doing anything but stand in the open doorway, her cigarette burning down to her fingers. It was almost as if she had detached herself from this situation altogether and had turned her mind to something else.

Holly bent down and gathered Casper up in her arms. He was pitifully light, like a bird's nest, and all she could feel through his pajamas were his ribs and his thighbones. He reeked of stale urine and fresh vomit.

"You put him down," said Mrs. Beale. "You hear me? You put him down."

"I'm taking him away from you, Mrs. Beale. I'm

going to drive him to the emergency room at East Portland and I'm going to save his life."

Casper rolled his eyes up to look at her. A string of dribble was swinging from his chin.

"I don't think so," said Mrs. Beale. "Casper is *my* child, and you can't take him off without my say-so." She threw her cigarette aside but still she made no move to stop Holly from carrying Casper away. Holly held Casper tightly, as tightly as she had ever held anyone.

"I'm taking him, Mrs. Beale, and nobody's going to prevent me."

"You think I won't sue you? I'll sue you."

"Mrs. Beale, you can do whatever you like, but Casper's survival comes first."

Holly turned and walked back down the drive, supporting Casper's prickly head against her shoulder. She was terrified that Mrs. Beale was going to come running after her and attack her from behind, but she kept on walking. When she reached her car and opened up the back door, she turned around to see that Mrs. Beale was still standing where she was before, lighting up another cigarette.

She climbed into her car, trembling. Casper said, "Where are you taking me?"

Holly helped him to fasten his seat-belt. "You'll see. Someplace where you can be happy."

A Celebration with "Mickey Slim"

When Holly arrived home, she made herself a glass of lemon tea and took it into her study. There was mail on her desk but she didn't feel like opening it. Her mind was too crowded with thoughts of Casper Beale. She had driven him to East Portland Memorial Hospital and they had immediately taken him into intensive care. She had reported what she had done to the police, and a very bullish woman detective had come to the hospital to ask her some questions. Under the circumstances, though, she hadn't thought that they would take the matter any further. "You should have done it by the book, honey, you know that. But you're not going to be prosecuted for saving a child's life."

She thought about Daniel Joseph, too, and Sarah-Jane Heilshorn, and the way in which Doug and Katie had let her down. She wasn't a bitter person. She wouldn't have been able to tolerate her deafness if she were bitter. But she felt deeply resentful about Doug's betrayal. He had used her as a scapegoat because she was deaf, and there was nothing she could do about it except despise him for it. All that bullshit about "the sweetest girl in the Children's Welfare Department."

Her cell phone vibrated.

"Meet me 6 pm Hugos Bar? Mickey."

Well, why not? she thought. She could use a drink, and a shoulder to cry on. It was 5:45 already, so she went to find her coat. Marcella was in the kitchen, ironing Daisy's blouses, and she said, "You going out, Ms. Summers? What time you come back?"

"Not late. But I've had one of those days."

"You don't worry. I always look after your Daisy."

Hugo's Bar was on Southwest Alder, a narrow building of chocolate-brown brick wedged between Esparto fashion store and a glossy new marble-front bank. Mickey was waiting for her right in back, at a circular oak table, under a low-suspended Tiffany-style lamp. All around the dark green walls hung mahogany-framed engravings of sternwheelers and steamboats.

He stood up when she arrived. He looked even more gaunt than usual. He said, "What'll it be?"

"A large glass of pinot noir. A *very* large glass of pinot noir."

"Something wrong?"

"I've been suspended. I quit."

He said, "You quit? I don't believe what I'm hearing." She told him all about Sarah-Jane Heilshorn, and he listened and nodded. When she had finished, her eyes were filled with tears of frustration, and he laid his hand on top of hers. "I always said Doug Yeats was an asshole, didn't I? Didn't I always say that? I'll bet when he was a kid he took an apple for his teacher every day, *and* polished it with his own nose perspiration."

"Oh God, make me feel sick."

"Well, don't you worry about Doug, because I've got some good news for you: We picked up two guys outside the Robert Herrera Hair Salon just after two o'clock this afternoon."

"Really?"

"Caught them in flagrante: They were trying to force Mrs. Gillian Rossabi into a four-by-four at the curbside. One of them was a well-known psychopath from Bend called Jimmy Novak and the other was a local waste of space called Frederick Drendel. Novak was carrying a .45, a pair of nylon handcuffs, and a switchblade knife."

"That's *terrific!* You actually got them! At least something's turned out good."

"Well, not totally good, not yet. We also arrested John H. Rossabi, Mrs. Rossabi's less-than-devoted husband, but Merlin Krauss contrived to be out when we called, although it's only a matter of time. I'm pretty confident we'll find your wood-pulp guy too."

Holly raised her glass. "Congratulations. Here's to you."

"Are you kidding me? We wouldn't have even known that this hit was going down at all if it hadn't been for you. Mrs. Rossabi would have been turned into cardboard boxes and nobody would have been any the wiser."

"Actually, they're not made of cardboard. They're made of linerboard with a corrugated medium sandwiched in between, one hundred percent recycled pulp."

Mickey frowned at her. "You're getting more like an encyclopedia every day, I swear it. What's the capital of Venezuela?"

They were still laughing and joking when Holly caught sight of somebody sitting in the booth on the opposite side of the bar, somebody so intensely black that they looked more like a shadow than a person. She couldn't see his face, because the Tiffany lamp hung in the way. All she could make out was a shoulder and an arm—or was it a cape and a hood? Or was it nothing but the way the light was falling across the buttoned banquette?

Mickey suddenly realized that she wasn't watching his lips.

"What's the matter? Something wrong?"

"I don't know. . . . Over in the corner there. Can you see somebody sitting there?"

"In the booth, you mean? No."

"You mean there's nobody there at all?"

He took another look and shook his head. "No. Nobody. Why?"

"I get the feeling that I'm being followed."

Mickey tipped back his whiskey. "Hasn't it ever occurred to you that you're more than worth following? I'd follow you myself, if I had the time."

Three Quiet Days

The next three days were so quiet that she felt as if time had stopped. She went shopping and bought herself two new sweaters at Pioneer Place, one rust-red and one navy. The rust-red sweater was too large when she tried it on at home so she had to take it back, and they didn't have a smaller one.

She sorted through her filing and shredded ten months' worth of credit-card bills and personal letters. She tidied the drawers in her bedroom, throwing away crumpled-up tubes of face cream and mascara brushes that looked like grumpy centipedes. She went out and bought three new imitation-leather photograph albums and emptied four shopping bags full of photographs onto the dining table so that she could shuffle them all into chronological order.

The trouble was, every photograph she picked up held her in a spell, and a whole afternoon went by before she had filled up even two and a half pages. Here was David, leaning against his new Porsche, grinning into the sunshine. Here was Holly, three weeks after his funeral, looking pale and cross. Here was Daisy, age eleven months, in nothing but a diaper, just about to topple sideways on the very first day when she started to walk.

And she thought to herself: *What was this all for? Why did I live through all of those years of love and argument and agony and loss? To end up here, jobless, alone, unloved, in this apartment, putting all these photographs in order?*

But she remembered then what George Greyeyes had told her about Raven. *Raven is a scavenger, who takes away your luck. First your livelihood, then your home, then your loved ones, and then your happiness.*

For the first time she acknowledged that she had been really cursed.

Casper's Warning

On Thursday evening she collected Daisy from school and took her to East Portland Memorial Hospital to visit Casper.

"Try not to be shocked, sweetheart: He looks very, very sick. But the doctors say that he's getting better."

Casper was out of intensive care, but he was still in a room of his own because he was so susceptible to infection. A small, bare room, with a view of the flat asphalt roof of the hospital kitchens, and the glaring sun going down over the Tualatin Mountains to the west.

Casper was propped up on three pillows, and he was being fed with a glucose drip. A dark fuzz was already growing on his head, and that made him look even more monkeylike than he had before. When she saw him, Daisy gripped Holly's hand and squeezed it tightly.

"Casper, this is my daughter, Daisy," said Holly, smiling. "How are you feeling today?"

Casper said, "Pretty tired, most of the time. I keep on falling asleep. Then I wake up and I don't know where I am."

"I talked to Dr. Arneson," Holly said. "He told me that you're doing real good. You've put on three and a half pounds since Monday."

Casper raised one of his bony hands and touched his cheek. "I keep wondering what it's going to be like, not being sick anymore."

"It's going to be a whole new life, believe me. Look, Daisy's brought you a present."

Daisy reached into her shopping bag and took out a scale-model Ferrari in a box. Casper looked at it and smiled. Then he handed it back.

"Go on, open it," said Daisy. "It's yours."

Casper looked up at Holly, and Holly suddenly realized that he had never been given any toys before—or if he had, he hadn't been allowed to keep them. He struggled to open the cellophane and in the end Daisy did it for him. He lifted up the car and peered into the windows. "It even has a steering wheel and a gearshift."

Holly said, "The doors open too."

They drew up chairs beside his bed and watched him as he steered the Ferrari over his bony knees.

After a while Holly said, "There's something I have to tell you, Casper: When you're better, you won't be going back home to live with your mother."

Casper frowned at her. "Why? Why not?"

"Because it was your mother who made you sick."

"I know. I know she did. But she always looked after me."

"Actually, she didn't. She deliberately starved you and she gave you medicine to make you vomit so that everybody would think you had cancer. She nearly killed you."

"Where am I going to go, then?"

"I expect that the Children's Welfare Department will find you some people to look after you. Foster parents. I don't work for them anymore, but I know for sure that they'll fix you up with some real nice people."

"But can't I go home?"

"I'm sorry. You won't be able to. But I wanted you to know that if you needed anybody to talk to . . . well, we'll always be here. Daisy and me."

Casper didn't say anything, but Holly could tell that he was upset. It happened so often when children were abused: No matter how badly they had been treated— even if they had been beaten or starved or sexually molested—they always wanted to go back to their parents. Children worked harder at keeping their family together than anybody did, and they always blamed themselves if the family fell apart.

"Casper . . . your mother isn't well. She wouldn't have treated you like that, otherwise."

"She always took care of me."

Holly didn't know what to say. She stood up and kissed Casper on his white, dry-skinned forehead. "Don't worry . . . things will work out. All you need to worry about is feeding yourself up. I want to see you eating cheeseburgers by the end of next week."

Casper's voice was suddenly different: throaty and almost threatening. "My momma . . . she won't like it if you take me away."

"I know she won't, Casper. But it's all for the best."

"Something bad will happen to you if you take me away. Something really, really bad."

"Why don't you get some rest? We'll come see you again in a couple of days."

Casper kept on staring at her, as if he were trying to remember every detail of what she looked like. As if he never expected to see her again.

They walked along the corridor to the elevator. Daisy said, "He's *creepy*."

"He's very sick, that's all."

"No," said Daisy, emphatically shaking her head. "He's *creepy*."

They crossed the hospital parking lot to Holly's car. As they did so, Holly saw Doug's green Pajero pull up outside the main entrance. Doug climbed out, although he didn't see Holly. He walked around and opened the passenger door. He helped out a woman in a brown suede coat.

Holly hesitated, holding her car keys in her hand. The woman turned around and she saw that it was Mrs. Beale.

Mrs. Beale hesitated, too, and looked around, as if she could sense that Holly wasn't far away. Just as Doug laid a hand on her shoulder to guide her inside, she caught sight of Holly and stared at her. As she did so, five or six black birds suddenly fluttered off the roof of the hospital and circled around, their feathers ruffled by the wind.

"Mommy?" asked Daisy.

"It's nothing," said Holly. "I thought I saw somebody I used to know, that's all."

In the Japanese Garden

Friday afternoon was sharp and sunny, so Holly drove up to the West Hills and went for a walk in the Japanese Garden, which had always been one of her favorite places to relax: five and a half intricate acres of pathways and bridges and stepping-stones that led between ponds and iris beds and formal gravel gardens. And Mount Hood, in the distant background, like Mount Fuji.

There was hardly anybody else around, and the fall sunshine glittered on the weeping willows. The chilly air was filled with the earthy smells of a gradually dying year. She walked through the five-tier stone lantern that led to the Strolling Pond Garden, and crossed the Moon Bridge over the upper pond. Farther down the garden, by the Zig Zag Bridge, she could see two Japanese men standing by the railings, talking, while a young Japanese girl of about fifteen was kneeling on one of the stepping-stones in the lower pond, wiggling her fingers in the dark green water to attract the koi carp.

Holly made her way down the mossy steps to the opposite side of the lower pond. Under the water the carp flickered like animated slices of orange peel. The girl looked up at her and smiled shyly. She wore a fleece-lined denim jacket and embroidered jeans and her hair was tied up in Pokémon-style bunches. Holly smiled back and gave her a little finger wave.

She sat down on a carved stone bench. She had needed an hour of reflection like this, a time to heal her hurt and her disappointment. She also felt that she had to make some decisions about herself. Was she really going to quit the Children's Welfare Department forever? How was she going to feel about all of those children out there who still needed her help? And what was she going to do about Mickey? Was she going to allow him to get closer? Did she trust him? Did she trust herself? She was always pleased when she saw him, and there was no question that she found him attractive, even though he wasn't handsome and even though she had witnessed how violent he could be.

She thought to herself: *You're afraid, aren't you? Why don't you stop being afraid? Next time you meet Mickey, show him that you're interested. See where it goes from there.*

A few curled leaves dropped from the trees onto the surface of the pond, circling around and around, and the carp came up to nibble at them. One of the Japanese men took off his white fedora and leaned forward on the railings, looking intently at the young girl.

"You don't think she'd give me any trouble?"

"Of course not. Her father brought her up to be obedient."

"Well, I could offer you a lot of money, depending on what she does. We have a new studio now, and a much more professional cameraman."

The man with the white fedora was about thirty-five, smartly dressed in a navy-blue blazer. The other man was about ten years older and dressed in a green weatherproof jacket. He took off his glasses and polished them on a crumpled shred of Kleenex.

"So how much are we talking about?"

"Two thousand. More, if the sales are good. She's pretty, and she's very young, and this time we hope to have more than thirty-five men."

The older man half-turned his back, so that Holly could no longer lip-read him, but she could still see the man with the white fedora. "It's our biggest seller now, *bukkake*. It outsells everything else we do by ten to one. I've even seen American *bukkake*."

Bukkake. Holly felt cold. Even here, in this tranquil Japanese garden, the world was poisoned. She hesitated for a moment, and then she stood up and walked around the edge of the pond until she came to the Zig Zag Bridge. The two men stopped talking, obviously waiting for her to pass. But she came right up to them, and smiled, and held up her cell phone.

"Pardon me, but I was wondering if either of you two gentlemen could help me. You see, my battery's dead and I have to call my daughter to tell her where to meet me."

"Ah," said the man with the white fedora. He reached into his blazer pocket and produced a tiny Sony cell phone with a shiny chrome cover. "Here, please, be my guest."

"That's so kind of you. I didn't know *what* I was going to do."

"Please, no problem."

Holly went across to the other side of the bridge and punched out Mickey's number. When he answered, she quickly texted him:

"NOTE THIS NO. HOLLY."

"??" he texted back.

"XPLN L8R."

Then she said loudly, "Okay, honey, I'll meet you at Janine's in fifteen minutes. That's great."

She handed the phone back. "Thanks again. Some people think I'm overprotective when it comes to my daughter . . . but you know, you can't be too careful, can you, not these days?"

"Absolutely right," agreed the older man.

"Is that your little girl down there?"

"My niece."

"Well, you must be very proud of her."

The two men exchanged a quick, enigmatic look. "I am," said the older man. "Very proud uncle indeed."

Text Message

In the parking lot she texted Mickey again and
explained what she had lip-read. She watched as the
girl and her uncle and the man in the white fedora
came out of the Japanese Garden and stood talking for
a while. Then the uncle and the man in the white fedora shook hands and bowed to each other before they
went off in opposite directions. The girl took hold of
her uncle's hand and swung it as she walked.

Mickey replied that the cell phone had already been
traced to Butterfly Motion Pictures with an address on
Boren Avenue in Seattle, Washington. "Ill put Det Nel-
son on it pronto." Holly wouldn't have known what
bukkake was unless she hadn't been involved in another
Japanese sex-abuse case last November, when more
than 60 *bukkake* videos had been confiscated from a
video rental store downtown. It was the latest rage in
Japanese pornography, in which dozens of men cli-
maxed over the upturned face of a single young girl
until she looked as if she had been frosted, like a cake.

Sometimes it was done with her eyes held wide open. Other times she was given pints of semen to drink, out of a flask, to see if she could manage to keep it all down. That was what the proud uncle on the Zig Zag Bridge had been offering for $2,000.

No Daisy

Holly drove home. The afternoon was growing overcast now. When she let herself in, Marcella was in the kitchen, rolling meatballs on a floured board.

"Hi, Marcella." She looked at the coatrack. "Daisy not back yet?"

Marcella shook her head. "Maybe she go to see her friend."

"She didn't say anything about it this morning. You couldn't give her a call for me, could you?"

"Sure thing." Marcella smacked the flour off her hands and picked up the phone from the kitchen wall. She dialed and waited, but after a while she shook her head. "Her phone is switch off."

"That's odd. She told me she'd be home by five for sure."

"Don't you worry, Ms. Summers. She forget what time it is, that's all."

Holly went to the window. "I don't want her out too late. . . . It looks like there's a hell of a storm coming over."

• • •

When the kitchen clock crept to six-thirty and Daisy still hadn't come back, Holly had Marcella call Daisy's best friend, Tracey Hunter. The sky was the color of slate, and raindrops began to measle the window-panes. Tracey's mother said that Daisy had left their apartment shortly after four and that as far as she knew she was coming directly home.

"I'm worried now," said Holly as Marcella hung up the phone. The Hunters lived only three blocks away, over the Columbia Valley Travel Office. "Try calling the Williamsons."

Marcella phoned all of the friends that Daisy might have gone to visit, but none of them had seen her. She also called Tyrone, in case she had stopped by the gallery, but he hadn't seen her, either. "But call me as soon as you find her," he said.

Holly put on her raincoat and said, "Listen . . . I'm going to go look for her. If she comes home just give me a buzz, okay?"

"Sure thing, Ms. Summers," said Marcella. "Don't forget your hat. It's a rain like drown rat."

When she stepped out into the street, the rain was cascading from the yellow-and-white-striped restaurant awning and flooding the gutters. People with umbrellas and newspapers over their heads were running for shelter. She turned up her collar, thrust her hands into her pockets, and stepped out quickly in the direction of the Hunters' home.

Halfway along Thirteenth Street she saw a small figure running toward her holding a pink cotton jacket over her head, and with relief she called out, *"Daisy!"*

But the figure wasn't Daisy at all; it was a little Chinese girl, and she ran past her without even looking at Holly.

With the rain clinging to her eyelashes and dripping from the tip of her nose, she walked all the way to the Columbia Valley Travel Office. There were color photographs in the window of all the different river trips that tourists could take up the Columbia and the Willamette, to Multnomah Falls and Mount Hood and the International Rose Test Garden, a mass of yellow roses. She looked around for a few moments, but there was no sign of Daisy anywhere, and she began to walk back.

She called into several stores and restaurants, asking if anybody had seen a little girl of eight in a pink jacket and jeans, but all she got in reply was the solemn shaking of heads. In the doorway of the Portland Family Bakery she sent a text message to Mickey, telling him what had happened.

His reply came back almost at once: "Don't worry Ill get on it go home."

Mickey Brings Bad News

She sat at the dining table, still wearing her wet raincoat, while Marcella stayed with her.

"I can't believe that she would have gone anywhere without telling me."

"Ms. Summers, Daisy is a good girl always, you know that. But even good girls sometimes play a little mischief."

"She's been upset lately, you know, about not having a father. I think she's getting to the age when she really needs a man in her life."

"Hmmh! That depends if *you* need a man in your life. You've been very good to Daisy, Ms. Summers, raised her good."

Holly tried to smile. "I don't know what I'd do without you, Marcella. I wish you'd call me Holly."

Marcella shook her head. "How many times you ask me this, hah? And each time what do I say? I work for you, I give you respect. In this times now, nobody give nobody no respect. Not husbands for wives, not parents for children. Every place you look is no respect."

• • •

A few minutes after eight-thirty, with still no sign of Daisy, the red light over the doorbell flashed, and Marcella went to answer it. It was Mickey, looking as if he had swum from the other side of the Willamette River.

"What's happened? Have you found her?"

Mickey glanced at Marcella. "I need to talk to you in private."

"You can trust Marcella."

"I know, but this is kind of tricky, and it's important for Daisy's sake that nobody else knows about it."

"Well . . . all right. Marcella, can you leave us alone for a while?"

"It's okay. I go downstairs and see Leo in the kitchen. You call me when you need me."

After Marcella had gone, Mickey said, "I had a call about twenty minutes ago from a snitch called Nicky Moranes. He said that Merlin Krauss had asked him to pass on a message."

"Merlin Krauss? A message? About what?"

Mickey took out a clean but fraying handkerchief and wiped his face and his neck. "It seems that Krauss has found out that you lip-read and that you're qualified to give evidence about what he was saying about knocking off Mrs. Rossabi. Don't ask me how he found out."

He took a deep breath, and then he said, "Holly, I'm afraid to say that he's taken Daisy and he's not going to give her back unless you guarantee that you won't testify against him in court."

Holly slowly sat down. She could actually feel her face turning to chalk. "He's *taken* her? Did he say where she was? Oh God, he hasn't hurt her, has he?"

"He said she was safe and well. But he wants to

meet you face-to-face and hear you promise that you're not going to help to convict him."

"Of course I will! Where is he?"

"Holly, it's not as easy as that. Merlin Krauss is wanted for conspiracy to commit homicide in the first degree—and now kidnapping. I don't have the authority to let you negotiate an amnesty for him. That's in addition to exposing a civilian to potentially mortal danger."

"But we're talking about Daisy's life! And you can't force me to testify against him, can you? And what kind of case will you have if I don't?"

"Holly, you're putting me in a real difficult position here."

"Difficult position? *Difficult position?* This is my little girl, Mickey! This is my dead husband's only child!"

"We're talking about a guy who arranges murders here, Holly! A guy who kills people for fun and profit! You think you can trust him to let Daisy go, and you too? If you go to see him, he'll probably whack you both!"

"I have to try, Mickey, and you have to let me. Tell me where he is."

Mickey shook his head. "This goes against any kind of kidnapping or hostage procedure."

"Who else knows about this? Your captain? Your commander?"

"So far . . . nobody but me."

"Then if nobody else knows about it, you won't have to take the responsibility for it, will you? All you have to do is tell me where Krauss wants to meet me."

"I'm sorry, Holly, I can't. I'm going to have to call this in and see what a negotiating team can do to get Daisy free."

Holly reached across the table and gripped his hand. "I'm begging you, Mickey: Help me. If Daisy gets hurt, then I wouldn't want to go on living anyway."

Mickey looked at her intently for a very long time. She saw something in his eyes but she couldn't understand what it was. Tension? Anxiety? Or relief? The artist Goya, who was suddenly struck deaf, had once said that it gave him the ability to see what was really there, and not what he was *told* to see.

"Okay," said Mickey at last, dry-mouthed.

"So where? Tell me where he is."

"He's in a house about five miles south of Bonneville, about an hour along the valley."

"How am I going to find it?"

Mickey stood up. "I'll take you there. You're under too much stress to find it yourself. Besides, if I come with you, you stand at least a half-decent chance of getting out of there in one piece."

"You don't know how much I appreciate this."

"Hey, I have a very soft spot for Daisy. I'm Uncle Mickey, remember?"

"Yes, you're Uncle Mickey."

He checked his watch. "Let me go first. . . . I'm parked around the corner by Kendrick's. It's very important that nobody knows that we left together."

"What shall I tell Marcella?"

"Tell her—I don't know—tell her that you called one of Daisy's friends and they think they know where she is. Tell her she can go home."

"Mickey . . . thank you."

"Yeah," he said. "Right."

Surprise Surprise

It started to thunder as they drove eastward on Interstate 84, along the Columbia River Valley. Holly couldn't hear it, but whenever the lightning flashed, she could see that the clouds were purple.

Mickey drove as fast as he could, but the rain was hammering down so hard that he could hardly see anything in the darkness up ahead of them, and when another car came toward them, the windshield was filled with brilliant spangles of blinding light.

Because it was so dark, it was difficult for them to have a conversation, but as they neared the Bonneville turnoff, Holly touched Mickey's arm. "What shall I say?" she asked him. Mickey turned to her so that she could see his lips in the light from the instrument panel.

"Don't volunteer anything. Just ask Krauss what he wants and tell him you agree. Don't challenge him. Don't lose your temper. Don't call him any names."

"I'm okay, Mickey. I've had to deal with worse people than Merlin Krauss."

"I don't think so. Not yet."

The road became a track and the forest all around them was as black as the forest in a fairy tale, where people wore dark cloaks and slippery shoes. Mickey's Aurora wasn't designed for off-road driving, and they jounced and jolted through puddles and potholes.

Mount Hood was so close now that Holly had to bend her head down to see it. Every now and then its snow-covered peak was lit up by oddly colored flashes of lightning.

"Ass end of noplace at all," said Mickey.

After nearly fifteen minutes, with branches and briers scraping at the car's paint, they turned up a sharp left-hand hairpin, and there stood a large cedar-built house on stone pillars with a wide deck outside. Eight or nine vehicles were parked outside, most of them luxury-edition Jeeps and Toyotas. The large windows of the house were all brightly lit, and as she climbed out of Mickey's car Holly could see people moving around inside.

"Merlin Krauss is holed up here? It looks more like a party than a hideout."

Mickey said nothing but took hold of her elbow and led her up the steps to the deck. As they approached the house, a patio door slid open and a young man appeared through the net curtains, holding a glass of sparkling wine in his hand. He was wearing a black turtleneck sweater and slacks, and at first Holly didn't realize who he was. But then he lifted his glass and said, "Mickey! You did it! You're a genius!"

He was the young lawyer whose lascivious conversation she had lip-read in the coffee shop in the court-house, the one who had admired her "gazongas."

Holly frowned at Mickey and said, "What's going on? What's *he* doing here?"

The young lawyer stepped back and gave her a mock bow, "Kenneth T. Mulgrew Junior, at your service, but just for tonight you can call me Kennie. Divorce settlements and prenuptial agreements a specialty, not necessarily in that order."

"Mickey, what the hell's going on? Where's Daisy? Where's Krauss?"

She tried to twist her elbow away but Mickey gripped it tightly. "Come on inside, Holly. There's some people who can't wait to meet you."

"Mickey—let go of me, you're hurting."

Mickey pulled her close to him. "Listen," he said, "this is not exactly what I said it was, but Daisy is still being held hostage, and if you don't behave yourself she's going to suffer, do you understand?"

"Mickey?" she said. "Mickey, what's going on here? Tell me!"

"It's a party, Holly, you were right. And you're the entertainment."

Kenneth T. Mulgrew took hold of her other arm, and between them they forced her through the patio doors and through the ghostly net curtains as if she were a bride appearing on her wedding day. She found herself in a large living room furnished with heavy leather-upholstered couches and chairs and with landscape paintings all around the walls. The room was crowded with at least a dozen men, almost all of whom she either knew or recognized. As she came through the curtains, they raised their glasses and cheered.

Over the racket, Holly turned to Mickey and said, "You have to tell me where Daisy is!"

"I'll tell you, don't you worry. But not just yet, okay?"

"Tell me where Daisy is!" she screamed, and the underwater sound of her voice momentarily silenced every man in the room.

Mickey gave her the smallest shake of his head. "She's safe, Holly, I promise you, and she's going to stay safe. But I had to think of some way to get you out here on a dark and stormy night, now, didn't I?"

Holly wrenched herself free of him and approached the assembly of men. They were all dressed in casual clothes, some of them in shiny Hugh Hefner–style bathrobes. Middle-aged, mostly, although there were one or two younger men. She looked from one to the other, and she simply couldn't believe that they were all here. Martin A. Brimmer, with his white cropped hair and his cleft chin, commander of the Central Precinct; Gerry Valdez, an Omar Sharif lookalike, deputy district attorney; Oliver Pearson, paunchy and perma-tanned, senior partner in one of the most respected law firms in Oregon, Pearson Greenbaum & Traske. Ranking police officers and court officials and even Randolph Bruckman, the charming and helpful legal adviser from the governor's office.

She looked from one to the other, but not one of them was at all abashed. Instead they smiled at her and lifted their wineglasses, and one or two of them winked. There was a heavy smell of aftershave in the room, Obsession and Hugo Boss, and an aromatic undertone of marijuana too.

"What's going on?" she said at last. "What's happening here? Gerry . . . Randolph . . . what are you all doing here? What have you done with my daughter?"

At that moment a white-haired man wearing a quilted black Japanese-style robe tied with a sash edged his way through from the back of the gathering. It was Judge Walter Boynton, who had always reminded her so much of Ray Walston in *My Favorite Martian*.

"Ms. Summers! So pleased you could come! I'll tell you what we're doing here: We're having ourselves a party. A surprise party, as far as you're concerned."

"I want my daughter back and I want her back now, and I want to go home."

"So what are you going to do? Call the police?"

Holly looked desperately to Mickey, but Mickey did nothing but give her a shrug. Why didn't he say something? Why didn't he *do* something?

Judge Boynton came up to her and tried to put his arm around her, but she stepped away. "Don't touch me. Take me back to Portland now and give me back my daughter."

"Well . . . that's not really an option, I'm afraid," Judge Boynton told her.

"If you want me to forget this ever happened, I'll forget it, I promise you. Just give me my daughter."

"In all fairness, no can do. We've kind of committed ourselves, haven't we? You know who we are now: You've seen our faces."

"But what do you want me for? What's this all about?"

Judge Boynton said, "Come here, let me show you something."

"What?"

"Come here, I won't touch you, I promise."

The other men stepped aside as he walked toward the window at the far end of the room. Holly looked around for any sign of sympathy or support, but all she got in return were the same shameless smiles.

Judge Boynton stood by the window. She could see his reflection, and hers, but she could also see beyond the parking area, where there was dark scrub and rocks, and a ghostly white figure that appeared to wave in the wind.

"You know what that is?" said Judge Boynton. "That's the spray from a waterfall, and whenever the wind gets up, it takes on the shape of a woman dancing. The Indians think that it's the spirit of Akula, the woman wonder-worker whose magic was so powerful that any man who crossed her was emasculated. That's why they call this place Phantom Woman Falls.

"It turned out to be very appropriate that I built a weekend house here, because my friends and I have been seeing for many years how women have been emasculating men in all walks of professional life, and in the judiciary in particular.

"These parties—they started as a way for us stuffed shirts in the legal profession to let our hair down. We called ourselves the Justice League, after the comic books. We used to hire a girl or two, drink a lot, do some fishing. But then one day one of our members complained about the way in which a woman in the Judicial Department had been promoted over his head, for no other apparent reason except that she was a woman.

"He said, 'I'd like to bring her out here for a weekend and show her what it's *really* like to get screwed.'

So . . . to cut a long story short, we fixed it for him."

Judge Boynton sipped his wine and smiled at the memory. "That's how it started. Instead of hookers, we brought high-flying women to our parties and, to put it simply, we gave them an object lesson in why God created women. To serve, and to be obedient, and to give pleasure whenever required."

Holly stared at him, appalled. "What happened to all these women?"

"What *happened* to them?" Judge Boynton didn't seem to understand the question.

"Oh my God," said Holly. She felt as if she couldn't breathe.

Judge Boynton said, "Believe me, if you're a good sport, you might even enjoy yourself. Now, why don't you relax, and have a drink, and we can all share an evening of grown-up entertainment."

"I'm leaving," said Holly. "Mickey, drive me back to Portland—and if you won't drive me back, give me your keys."

Mickey took off his coat and flung it over the back of an armchair. Then he unbuttoned his cuffs. "Holly . . . my whole life I've been rejected or insulted or looked down on by the women I really want. . . ."

"*What?*" Holly stared at him in disbelief. She thought that she must have made some ridiculous misinterpretation in reading his lips. But he came right up to her, standing so close that she could feel his breath on her face.

"It means that I've had enough, like all of my friends here have had enough." He pronounced his words very slowly and clearly, so that there was no mistake.

"*Mickey?*" She felt like hitting him with her fists in frustration. This couldn't be Mickey, talking like this. Not the Mickey who told Daisy a bedtime story. Not the Mickey who had brought her lilies. And to think she had sat in the Japanese Garden only this afternoon and thought about starting an affair with him. She almost felt as if she were going mad.

"I *want* you," he said. "I know for sure that Kennie wants you; and Mark; and Randolph; and so what we're going to do is: We're all going to have you. You can make this easy and decide that it's going to happen anyhow, so you might as well have a good time. Or else you can make it difficult, and if you make it difficult, the odds are that one or two of us might have to slap you to get you in line."

"Mickey, for God's sake, tell me this is some kind of joke."

"No joke, baby. This is where the guys and me get what life has denied us."

"You said you liked me. You said you *loved* me."

"I *do* love you, Holly, don't doubt it. I've loved you ever since I first saw you standing at that barbecue with those two hot dogs, one in each hand, wondering what the hell to do with them. I always flirted with you, didn't I? I always took care of you, didn't I? Fetched and carried? But what did I ever get in return? A peck on the cheek and a plateful of pork and peppers."

"Mickey, don't. Please, Mickey. This isn't you."

Mickey gave her a slanting, Harrison Ford–playing-a-psychopath smile. "Sorry, Holly. I've never really been the sympathetic sort. *Patient,* maybe, when patience is called for. Sometimes you can get what you want by knocking somebody's teeth out. But other times you have to play it more subtle. Like fly-fishing, you know? Casting, waiting, and reeling them in. And that's what I've been doing to you: casting, waiting, and reeling you in. And here you are, landed."

"You're not going to . . . ," Holly began, but everything was rapidly beginning to make sense. *This* was why she had been feeling that the world around her had altered so much, and that bad luck was sniffing so close to her heels. She hadn't been able to understand what was wrong, but of course it had been much too close to her, so close that she couldn't focus on it. It had been Mickey all the time. His lips had said that he loved her but his eyes had been watching her with nothing but dispassion. A raven's eyes. A predator's. In a way, it was worse than discovering that he had been killed.

"God, you're evil," she said.

"No," said Mickey. "Just tired of you treating me like some kind of second cousin." Before she could stop him, he ducked his head down and kissed her forehead. "You're mine now. You're *ours*."

She swallowed. The men all shuffled in closer now, still smiling. When she spoke, her throat was so constricted that she couldn't stop herself from coughing. "If I"—cough—"if I let you do this . . . will you swear to me that nothing will happen to Daisy?"

Judge Boynton beamed and lifted his glass. "Now, that's one of the things that I really like in a woman: maternal instinct."

Raven's Revenge

"This is the arena," announced Judge Boynton proudly, leading the way into the bedroom. In the center of the room stood a four-poster bed with carved pine pillars and headboard, hung with heavy orange-and-gold brocade curtains and covered with a matching throw. The floor was carpeted in cream shag pile, and on the walls hung a series of erotic oil paintings that might have been titled *Nudes of All Nations*. It looked as if it had been designed for a *Playboy* spread, circa 1973.

Mickey ushered Holly into the room. Close beside her, Martin A. Brimmer said, "Forget about your inhibitions, Holly. This is a special place. Private. Nobody else will ever find out what happened here."

"This is nothing to do with inhibitions," Holly retorted. "This is nothing but gang rape by a group of losers who are too old and too ugly to find a woman who wants to go to bed with them."

"Holly," warned Mickey. "We're thinking of Daisy now, aren't we?"

"Oh, sorry, Uncle Mickey. And to think I let you sit on her bed and tell her a bedtime story . . ."

"That was a story about somebody who did somebody else a favor—and got rewarded for it."

"That was a story about men who get what they want by deception, and if they can't get it by deception, they get it by force."

"Come on, now, Holly," put in Randolph Bruckman. "We're all friends here, aren't we?"

"How can you call yourself a friend?"

Randolph gave her a private little smile. "To tell you the truth, I've always wanted to ask you out to dinner. Never had the nerve, I guess."

"Well, this will save you the price of a meal, won't it?"

It was then, however, that Judge Boynton said, "Okay, gentlemen. Let's do it."

Mickey and Martin seized Holly's arms while another man came up behind her and tried to gag her with a silk scarf. She kicked and struggled and thrashed her head from side to side, but two other men grabbed her legs and they were far too strong for her. Mickey seized her chin and held it in a clamplike grip while the scarf was pulled tight between her teeth and fiercely knotted at the back of her head. She stared at Mickey with bulging eyes, trying to appeal to him to stop these men from hurting her and to let her go. "*Unnnffffff!*" she grunted at him, but all he did was grin and turn away. The next thing she knew, a dark woolen scarf was tied over her eyes so that she was blinded as well as deaf.

She was suddenly swamped in total helplessness and

absolute terror. She felt as if she had been swept away from the shore by an icy wave, in darkness, and that she was drowning, with nobody to see her and nobody to hear her. She had always been able to cope with her deafness, because she could still see, but her blindness made her deafness even more overwhelming than ever.

She was going to die. Her whole world was cold and black and chaotic but utterly soundless. She couldn't even manage a muffled scream, and if she had, she couldn't have heard it. It had been frightening enough when she was a child, seeing Margaret fall from her bedroom balcony in flames, but now death was after *her*, and she had never realized how heart-clenchingly terrifying it was going to be, to know that the end of her life had almost arrived.

Her arms were forcibly lifted and her sweater was pulled over her head. Her bra catch was unfastened by fumbling fingers. She violently twisted her hips, but two men unbuttoned her jeans and dragged them down to her ankles, and at last her panties were pulled down too.

She had no idea of what the men were saying—whether they were silent or whether they were laughing or whether they were whooping with excitement. She was so panicky now that she found it difficult to breathe, but there was no way of begging them to stop.

She was heaved across the bed. Four or five men turned her over onto her back, raising her arms over her head and opening her legs. They held her pinned down until she felt narrow nylon cords being tied around her wrists and ankles, leaving her spread-eagled and helpless.

She thought: *Now, now they're going to do it,* and braced herself, biting hard on her gag.

But then there was a long pause. Thirty seconds went by . . . almost a minute.

What are they doing? Maybe they've changed their minds. No, they haven't changed their minds. They're going to rape me and then they're going to kill me. They'll have to kill me, won't they, because I know who they are. Oh God, I hope they don't do the same thing to Daisy. Please don't let them hurt Daisy.

She tried to calm herself by breathing deeply and steadily, the way her yoga instructor had shown her, but it was almost impossible with her mouth so tightly gagged. She kept swallowing saliva, almost choking.

Still nothing happened; none of the men touched her. She lay completely still, trying to feel them, trying to sense what they were doing. Were they still in the room? Maybe they *had* changed their minds. Maybe they would let her go if she promised not to tell anybody what had happened here tonight.

But she knew with iron-cold certainty they wouldn't. How could they? A judge, a police commander, several respected attorneys, a police lieutenant, and a court official.

How could they afford to let her live?

Judge Boynton had boasted that none of their previous victims had complained, and there could be only one reason for that. She thought of Sarah Hargitay and Jennie McLellan and Kay Padowska and Helena Carlsson. All of them independent, strong, and very attractive women, and all of them had disappeared without a trace, except for Sarah Hargitay's shoe, which had been discovered at Bridal Veil, only a few miles from here.

Oh God, Daisy. Oh God, let them do what they like to me but don't let them kill me. What will little Daisy do if they kill me?

Holly felt something soft and heavy touch her cheek, like plums. Instantly she jerked her face away, but then something else brushed her other cheek, something harder, and then her shoulder. She felt a man climb onto the bed beside her, then another, and another. She could feel them, she could feel their weight and she could feel the heat of their bodies, and she could smell them too: a strong, rank smell, stale sweat and Gucci aftershave and alcohol. They were all naked, all of these men, all hairy, and they were rolling and massaging their penises all over her body, even the soles of her feet, as a way of exciting themselves.

Wildly she kept on jerking her head from side to side, but that only encouraged them to press their penises against her even harder. Even though she was tied so tightly, she managed to twist her hips and buck herself up and down on the bed, but again that only seemed to excite the men even more.

She felt warm slime against her left cheek, and she was so disgusted that she retched. She knew that she couldn't break free, but she wasn't going to let them think that she was ever going to give in to them. She was trembling uncontrollably with effort and she could feel the blood banging inside her head, but she kept on struggling and grunting and more than anything else her soul screamed out, *No!*

Fingers started to stray all over her, tugging at her nipples and sliding right inside her, single fingers at first, then three and four fingers at a time. There was nothing she could do but shake her head and let out furious noises, like an animal.

Oh God, let this be over. Oh, please, God, let this be over.

There was another pause. She tried to catch her breath again, but the smell of sexually aroused men was so repulsive that she gagged again, and bile ran down the back of her throat. Then a heavily built man climbed onto the bed and positioned himself between her legs. She could feel his hairy thighs against her skin. He opened her up with his fingers, and then she felt the swollen head of his penis pressing against her.

Please God.

Something happened—something so jumbled and unexpected that she couldn't work out what it was. The man bounced on the bed and struggled off her urgently, as if he had found a snake in the sheets. Some of the other men started to struggle around too: She felt three or four of them collide with the side of the mattress. She couldn't imagine what was going on, but they all seemed to have totally lost interest in their orgy in a matter of seconds.

She thought she faintly saw two or three flashes through her blindfold, and then she smelled something smoky and acrid. *Don't tell me the house is on fire and they've just left me here, all tied up,* she thought. She grunted and pulled at the ropes around her wrists, but the men had knotted them so tight that she couldn't even begin to loosen them.

Then she felt a hand placed on top of her head,

firmly but very gently, as if somebody were trying to re-assure her to stay calm. Her head was lifted from the pillow and the blindfold tugged free.

To her surprise, the house was in darkness, except for a dim illumination from the windows. A shape was standing over the bed, something huge and very black. She stared up at it, still gagged, unable to cry out. Her heart almost melted with fear. This was a hundred times more frightening than the Justice League. This was the thing that took all of your happiness away. This was bad luck incarnate, and now it had caught up with her at last, and it was greedy for her misery.

Outside the bedroom window the lightning flickered on the peak of Mount Hood, and she saw black shiny feathers and eyes that glittered in the darkness like beetles.

Another black shape appeared in the doorway, and then another. The lightning flickered again. She should have known that the mountain would eventually draw her to her death.

It was then, though, that her gag was untied, and one of the black shapes approached the foot of the bed. She saw a knife shine, and her ankles were released, quickly followed by her wrists. The huge black figure picked her up off the bed and wrapped the throw around her.

Only a second later all the lamps came back on again, and Holly found herself sitting on the bed next to George Greyeyes. He was dressed in a black leather jacket, but the black gleam that she had imagined were feathers were simply his greased-back hair. At the end of the bed, folding up his jackknife, was another Indian whom she didn't recognize. He was twentyish, broad-faced, good-looking, with a plaid shirt that didn't conceal his bodybuilder physique. A third young Indian appeared, slighter and skinnier, with glasses and with a leather tool pouch attached to his belt.

George Greyeyes took hold of Holly's hand. "Are you okay? Look: Your clothes are all here. Why don't you get dressed?"

She nodded, numbly. "Oh, George. Oh, God. They were going to—"

"Shh, everything's okay now. But we have to get out of here."

Holly stared at him. She still couldn't quite believe what had happened. "I have to find Daisy."

"Daisy's fine. Apparently somebody nabbed her while she was walking home and drove around with her for a couple of hours. But after that, they dropped her back at the end of the street, safe and sound."

"How did you find me? How did you know what they were going to do to me?"

"Shh," said George. "Let's leave that till later. We'll give you a couple of minutes to get dressed and then we have to go."

"I thought you were Raven. I really did."

"If it hadn't been for Raven, I may not have found you. But come on, hurry."

When she was dressed, she went back through to the living room. There was blood sprayed everywhere, all up the walls, all over the furniture. Judge Boynton lay facedown on one of the leather couches, white and skinny like a Roswell alien, with most of the back of his head blown off. Randolph Bruckman was folded up in the corner with a hole in his big hairy belly. Three other men lay dead and naked in the kitchen doorway, a tangle of arms and legs.

"Mickey Slim" was close to the open patio door, facedown, his steel-colored eyes wide open, as if he were making a microscopic inspection of the carpet. Blood crept out from underneath his chest.

Holly slowly approached him. She stood over him with her hand pressed over her mouth while George Greyeyes kept a cautious eye on her.

Mickey's arms were dotted with dozens of small circular scars, pale and wrinkled, and his back was decorated with faded white ridges. These weren't the kind of scars that a cop would sustain on the streets. They hadn't come from bullets or knives or gangland beatings. But Holly knew what they were. Holly had seen marks like them so many times before, only fresher, on the arms and backs of children whose parents had stubbed out cigarettes on them and lashed them with belts and canes.

When he was small, Mickey must have suffered the same misery as Daniel Joseph and countless other children. Now she knew the real reason why he had knocked out Elliot Joseph's teeth.

She hesitated for a moment. She didn't know whether she felt anger or pity. Then she said, "What about the rest of them?"

"Run off into the woods, bare-ass naked," said the Indian boy in the plaid shirt, with a grin.

"What are you going to do? God, George, you've *killed* them! Aren't you going to call the police?"

"These people *are* the police. And the judiciary too. What do you seriously think is going to happen here?"

"I don't know. I really don't know. But I think I'd like to go home now, if I can."

George laid his arm around her shoulders and gave her a squeeze. "You sure opened a can of worms here, Holly. But all that's going to happen is that somebody's going to put the lid back on, real tight."

They left the house and went down the steps. George's Grand Cherokee was waiting for them there, and George helped Holly into the front passenger seat. She turned and looked back, and as she did so a lurid flash of lightning lit up the peak of Mount Hood, as if it were a stage set for a melodramatic play.

Superstition

George came to see her two days later. Marcella had pot-roasted a chicken with red vinegar and they opened a bottle of Barolo.

"So what did the police say?" asked Holly, tearing off a piece of bread to mop up the juice on her plate.

"They said that I was clearly acting in self-defense and that no charges are going to be pressed."

"They said that straight-faced?"

"Yup."

"They said it was self-defense despite the fact that you shot a judge and three other men in the judge's own home, and they were all naked, and none of them were armed?"

"To be fair, somebody fired off one shot at us first. I guess it was probably Mickey. Anyhow, you know what my father always used to say? The law is only a point of view."

"Have you heard any more about the rest of them?"

"Still running around the Mount Hood Recreation Area in their birthday suits, living off nuts and berries, I imagine."

"What's 'birthday suits'?" asked Daisy.

"Naked," said George. "But then some people have *no* shame at all."

Holly said, "I still can't work out how you found me . . . how you saved me."

George smoothed back his hair. "This is really tasty, this chicken. Your Marcella ought to give me the recipe."

"Go on, George. Tell me."

"I'm a little embarrassed, because this makes me sound so superstitious. But I wouldn't have found out what had happened to you if I hadn't believed in Raven."

"When you say *believed,* you mean *really* believed?"

"I believed in that curse that Elliot Joseph cast on you too. After he did that, I made a special point of checking up on you, even following you sometimes, just to make sure that Raven wasn't close behind you."

"You really thought that Raven would come to get me?"

"In a way, he did, didn't he? He brought you plenty of bad luck. But those times I was following you, I began to notice that other people were watching you, too, and other people were checking up on your movements. That lawyer that asked me about you, I caught him talking to his friends about you later, and the way they were talking I began to think that something very strange was being set up. I didn't tell you because I didn't really have any evidence, and you were jumpy enough anyway, thinking that every black shadow you saw was Raven coming closer."

"Raven tapped at my bedroom window," said Daisy.

"Well, if he did, he was only trying to warn you. Raven only brings misery to those who are cursed, not their children."

"So what happened on Friday evening?" asked Holly.

"I was having a drink with John Singing Rock and his brother Henry after work, in the Pioneer Bar. We'd had a pretty hard day and I needed to relax. But who should I see on the other side of the bar but this young lawyer guy, and he was talking to two of his friends. He was really excited, really up. He said that Mickey Kavanagh was going to collect you from your home and drive you to Phantom Woman Falls, and that they were all going to"—he glanced at Daisy—"well, they were all going to make whoopee."

"What's whoopee?" Daisy wanted to know.

"It's fun, like having a party."

"So what's a whoopee cushion?"

"That's fun too. It's a cushion that makes a farty noise when you sit on it."

"Can you buy me one?"

"Believe me, pumpkin, from what Marcella tells me, you don't need one."

She turned back to George. "You *followed* us? Me and Mickey?"

George nodded. "It wasn't easy, in that storm, believe me. When we got there, we looked in the window, saw what was going on, and Henry went down to the basement and killed the generator."

"You saved my life, George. You know what they would have done to me, don't you?"

"I don't think it takes too much imagination."

She leaned across and kissed his cheek. "Thank God you're deaf as well . . . otherwise you never would have known what those guys in the Pioneer Bar were saying."

After Daisy had been tucked into bed, they spent the rest of the evening talking by candlelight. Holly told George how Mickey had tricked her into going to Phantom Woman Falls by pretending that she was going to do a deal with Merlin Krauss.

"Didn't you see it on the news?" said George. "The highway patrol arrested Krauss just outside Klamath Falls. Yesterday morning, I think—for speeding. They say they're close to arresting the guy who was supposed to dispose of the body too. It looks like you're going to have your day of glory in court after all."

They also discussed the Joseph case. Little Daniel was improving, although he would never regain the sight of his left eye, and his speech was slurred. George had heard nothing about the Heilshorn case except that Anthony Heilshorn had mysteriously managed to break both of his legs on his second day at the North County Correctional Facility.

A Present from Ned

George had just opened another bottle of wine when the red light over the doorbell flashed. "Somebody's calling late," he said. "Do you want me to get it?"

"No, that's all right. Just pour out the wine. It's probably Marcella, forgotten something. She'll forget her head one day."

She went downstairs and opened the front door. A man in a brown coat was standing outside with a large bunch of yellow roses.

"Holly Summers?" he asked.

"That's me."

"Present from Ned," the man said. He lifted the bunch of roses and shot her in the face at point-blank range, in an explosive shower of yellow petals.

Not sure
what to
read next?

Visit Pocket Books online at
www.SimonSays.com

Reading suggestions for
you and your reading group

New release news

Author appearances

Online chats with your favorite writers

Special offers

And much, much more!

10421